ATL

SEA

VENEZUELA

GUIANAS

COLOMBIA

UADOR

P E R U

A N D E S   MTS

B R A Z I L

BOLIVIA

PARAGUAY

O C E A N

A R G E N T I N A

A N D E S   MTS

C H I L E

Pampas

URUGUAY

Patagonia

A T L A N T I C   O C E A N

SHRINERS HOSPITAL SCHOOL PROGRAM

LATIN AMERICAN TALES

From the Pampas to the Pyramids of Mexico

LATIN AMERICAN TALES

From the Pampas to the Pyramids of Mexico

By Genevieve Barlow

Illustrated by William M. Hutchinson

RAND McNALLY & COMPANY
Chicago · New York · San Francisco

For My Pupils

1772

Contents

The Enchanted Palace   9

The Fox Who Wanted to Whistle   18

The Lazy Fox   23

The Strange Adventures of Alcavilu   28

The Gift of the Moon Goddess   38

The White Spider's Gift   43

The Great White Condor   50

The Little Frog of the Stream   57

The Fox and the Mole   62

The Search for the Magic Lake   68

The Tree Goddess   82

The Magic Eagle   89

The Disobedient Giant   97

Mister Frog's Dream   104

How the Porcupine Outwitted the Fox   113

The Peacock and the Puhuy   119

The Sacred Amulet   126

The Cuckoo's Reward   134

Bird Cu   138

AUTHOR'S NOTE

These stories have been translated from the Spanish, re-written, and freely adapted from the following sources:

The Enchanted Palace and *The Magic Eagle* from "Leyendas de los Andes" by Rafael Morales (Madrid, Aguilar, S.A. de Ediciones, 1959)

The Fox Who Wanted to Whistle and *The Lazy Fox* from "Antología Folklórica Argentina para las Escuelas de Adultos" (Buenos Aires, Guillermo Kraft LTDA, 1940)

The Strange Adventures of Alcavilu from "Leyendas y Cuentos Araucanos" by Blanca Santa Cruz Ossa (Valparaiso, Universo, 1938)

The Gift of the Moon Goddess from "Leyendas Guaraníes" by Ernesto Morales (Buenos Aires, Ateneo, 1929)

The White Spider's Gift from "La Leyenda del Ñandutí" by Francisco Barnoya Galvez (Santiago de Chile, Empresa Editora Zig-Zag, S.A., 1939)

The Great White Condor, from "Leyendas de mi Tierra" by Antonio Díaz Villamil (La Paz, Bolivia, Editorial "Renacimiento" de Flores, San Román y Cía, 1929)

The Little Frog of the Stream and *The Fox and the Mole,* from "Leyendas y Fábulas Peruanas" by Enriqueta Herrera Gray (Lima, Peru, 1945)

The Disobedient Giant and *The Sacred Amulet* from "Leyendas del Caribe" by Rafael Morales (Madrid, Aguilar, S.A. de Ediciones, 1959)

7

The Peacock and the Puhuy and *The Cuckoo's Reward,* from "El Alma Misteriosa del Mayab" by Luis Rosado Vega (México, Ediciones Botas, 1957)

Bird Cu from "Cuentos y Leyendas de México" by Alfredo Ibarra, Jr. (México, D.F., Academia Nacional de Historia y Geografía, Sociedad de Folklórica de México, 1941)

The following never-before-published legends were told to the author during her travels through Latin America, from 1938 through 1964:

The Search for the Magic Lake, as told in Quito, Ecuador

The Tree Goddess, as told in Bogota, Colombia

Mister Frog's Dream, as told in Managua, Nicaragua

How the Porcupine Outwitted the Fox, as told in Tegucigalpa, Honduras

The Enchanted Palace

A TALE TOLD BY THE TEHUELCHE INDIANS OF PATAGONIA

Thousands of Tehuelche Indians once made their home on the cold, windy plains of southern Argentina, known as Patagonia. Patagonia is a bleak and barren plateau. Its geographical limits have never been fixed by law or even by common usage, but the area is generally known to be the land south of the Pampas, lying between the Andes and the Atlantic Ocean. Because the climate in most of Patagonia is too cool and too dry for raising crops, the Tehuelche Indians existed chiefly on guanacos, ostrich eggs, armadillos, wild potatoes, and roots similar to parsnips. It wasn't until the Spaniards brought sheep to Argentina that the Tehuelches became sheepherders. Up to that time, the only domesticated animal was a native dog that resembled the Scotch Terrier. The Tehuelche Indians were known for their tall stature. They were not warlike, but lived in small bands composed of relatives and close friends. They hunted together for the fox, guanaco, and wild cat, using only the bow and arrow. There are now only about one thousand Tehuelche Indians still wandering as shepherds over the barren plains of Patagonia.

An old Indian shepherd, named Taycho, lived on the cold, grassy plateau of Patagonia in Argentina. Taycho felt a great longing in his heart. He wanted to walk to the mighty Andes and gaze up at their snowy peaks. He wished to explore the forest and lakes that lay at the base of these majestic mountains.

One day Taycho said to his wife, "Now that the sheep are grazing close to home, could you care for them while I travel to the great mountains? It will be for only a short while."

"Of course, I shall gladly tend the sheep. But please don't go near the mountains."

"I am sure of foot, and wild animals are few, so what do you fear?"

The wife began to weep fearfully. "Have you forgotten the warnings of our childhood? Surely you must remember that the invisible ones live there, ready to bewitch any visitor."

Taycho laughed good-naturedly. "Dear wife, I do not fear people I cannot see. You speak of an old superstition that I do not believe."

Reluctantly, the wife gave her consent. Taycho, eager to be on his way, set out the following daybreak, promising to return soon.

His heart was filled with joy as he trudged toward the beckoning peaks. Everything was new and wonderful to him. There were strange birds nesting on the ground, for there were no trees in this rocky region. Unknown flowers, bright as a rainbow, covered the fields, and the air was filled with sweet smells from plants crushed beneath his feet.

One night Taycho was sleeping in a cave. He was aroused by the sound of voices and singing. He sat up, looked around, and called out. There was no answer.

"It must have been a dream or the whistling of the wind," Taycho said aloud. "No one lives here, or comes to this lonely spot, and I certainly don't believe in the invisible ones."

But all at once he recalled his wife's warning, and he felt a sudden fear.

Early the next morning, as he prepared his food, a voice came from the entrance to the cave. "Good morning, friend."

Taycho turned. There was no one to be seen at the cave door.

"Aren't you going to answer us?" a woman's voice inquired.

Taycho was surprised. "Where are you? To whom am I speaking?" he asked.

A third voice answered, "We are your friends, and we are here beside you."

"But I cannot see you," Taycho exclaimed.

"It is not meant for you to see us," the first speaker replied. "But so you may know you are with friends, we want you to have this gift."

At that moment, a leather pouch fell at the shepherd's feet.

"It is for you. Open it," the strange voice urged.

Taycho obeyed.

He opened the drawstring and looked into the pouch. He gasped in surprise! It was filled with precious stones of many colors.

"Is this really for me?" he asked in wonderment.

"Yes, it is, friend. It is to prove our friendship. Now, Taycho, will you come to our palace and visit us?" asked a voice.

Taycho had not time to answer, for at that moment a mist arose, then dissolved. There, before him, stood a gleaming palace, decorated with gold, silver, and precious jewels.

"Come this way! Follow us!" the voices sang in chorus.

Taycho could not resist the temptation to follow. He entered through a great, golden doorway, and came into the palace.

As if under a spell, Taycho followed the voices. Then he heard the giant door close behind him with a loud CLANG.

Taycho was panic-stricken. He rushed against the door, trying to open it. But it was in vain.

"Do not be afraid, Taycho. Because you have lived a long and good life we mean to honor you," said a deep voice. "Only once in a thousand years do we find a mortal who is worthy to be a guest within the walls of our kingdom. We would like you to remain with us a few days and tell us about the world beyond the great Andes. You may leave whenever you wish."

There, before him, stood a gleaming palace

Taycho, now unafraid, stayed and told his unseen hosts about his daily life and the ways of his tribe.

How happy he was in this beautiful palace where he was treated like a royal visitor! He wandered about the great halls and through the gardens filled with rare and fragrant flowers. He gazed in wonder at the singing birds with gay plumage and at the graceful swans swimming in the many pools. Although he enjoyed the sights and the delicious food, he saw no other persons and he grew lonely for the company of his good wife.

After several days had passed, Taycho said, "Dear unseen friends, tomorrow I must leave. Already I have been away from my dear wife too long."

"Your wife is well, Taycho. Stay with us a while longer," a voice beseeched him.

Taycho thanked his hosts, but insisted that he should leave. So early the next morning he stood at the palace door, and waited eagerly for it to open.

"We are sorry to see you go, Taycho," said a voice at his side. "You have given us great pleasure with your companionship and your tales. Here, at your feet, is our parting gift."

Taycho stooped down and picked up a handsome golden vase. It was brimming with diamonds, rubies, and pearls. The voice cautioned, "You must never tell anyone about us or about your visit to our palace. If you do, great misfortune will come upon you."

"I promise I shall not. And my thanks for your kindness. Now may I please leave?"

Taycho brought out the treasure and showed it to her

With these words the door was flung open. As it closed behind him, Taycho turned for a last look at the palace. It had disappeared. Only sand and dry brush grew in its place.

At last Taycho reached home. His wife was overjoyed to see him safe and sound. "It is nearly a year since you left, dear husband. I have worried about you every day. Tell me where you have been."

"A year!" Taycho interrupted with astonishment. "I

regret the trouble I have caused you. Please forgive me. I was on a great adventure near the Andes, and I had no idea that so much time had passed." His tone of voice and the look in his eyes forbade further questioning.

For many days, Taycho kept his promise to the invisible ones. But then his wife began to question him about his journey. When he refused to tell, she pouted and sulked, moaned and wept.

Taycho softened when he saw his wife's tears. He told her the true story. He brought out the treasure that he had hidden in his poncho, and showed it to her.

"Dear wife," Taycho ended dejectedly, "now I have broken my promise to the invisible ones, and I fear I may be punished."

"Do not fear," the wife replied, although she, too, was frightened. "I shall keep your secret."

Some days later, while the wife was admiring the precious jewels, two women of her tribe entered the house unexpectedly.

"Where did you get these jewels?" one exclaimed.

"I cannot tell," the wife answered.

The women soon left, but this was the beginning of much trouble for Taycho and his wife.

That evening the chieftain appeared at Taycho's home. "Tell me the story of the jewels," he demanded, "or I shall condemn you and your wife to death."

Trembling with fear, Taycho related the story of his visit with the invisible ones. Then he displayed the gifts that he had received from them.

The chieftain did not believe Taycho's story. "I shall see if you are telling me the truth. Tomorrow I am leaving for a visit with the invisible ones."

The chieftain arrived at the cave where Taycho had slept. He stayed two days and two nights, but he heard no voices. Then, just when he was about to leave for home, a mist rose. As it disappeared, the beautiful palace stood before him.

He ran to the closed door and shouted, "I am a chieftain. Let me in!"

A voice answered, "Only once in a thousand years do we entertain a mortal. Our last guest left a short time ago."

Before the chieftain could speak again, the palace disappeared. For days he remained there, hoping to hear a voice, or to see the palace again. But it did not reappear.

Finally the chieftain returned home. He called Taycho to him and said, "You told the truth about the invisible ones and the palace."

Taycho shook his head sadly and said, "I am glad you believe me, but after you left, I was punished for breaking my promise. All of my treasures have disappeared, except this golden vase which now is empty. I do not deserve to keep it. You may have it, if you wish."

The chieftain reached out his hand. The vase disappeared in the air.

All this happened long years ago, and no one has ever again seen the enchanted palace.

The Fox Who Wanted to Whistle

A TALE TOLD IN ARGENTINA

More than anything else in the world the fox wanted to whistle like the partridge. Every day he leaned back against his den wall to practice. He pursed his lips together and blew his breath between his sharp teeth. Out came a whooshing sound from the front and sides of his mouth. Again and again he tried, often taking such deep breaths that his chest bellowed out like a furry balloon.

Now, although the sound he made was not at all pleasant, the fox smiled to himself broadly and exclaimed, "How well I am learning!"

One day as he was giving himself a whistling lesson, the puma passed by.

"Good day, friend fox," he said, "what is wrong? Are you sick?"

The fox was highly indignant.

"No, I am not sick!" he fairly shouted. "Can't you see I am only practicing?"

"What are you practicing?" asked the puma, who had meanwhile climbed a nearby tree.

"Whistling," replied the fox. "Listen to this."

"Whistling," replied the fox. "Listen to this"

He took a deep, deep, breath and opened his mouth so one could barely see his teeth. He lifted his sharp muzzle skyward and let loose such a horrible sound that the puma lay back his ears and hunched in his head.

"You are a creature of many talents . . ." began the puma tactfully. Then, from the safety of his perch, he laughed at the fox and added, ". . . but whistling isn't one of them!"

The hair on the fox's back bristled. As soon as he regained his composure, he answered the puma with a confident air, "Oh yes it is! Some day I am going to whistle like the partridge. She has the most beautiful whistle of any bird in the forest."

"Then why don't you ask her to teach you?" asked the puma. "But you'll have to promise not to eat her," he warned. "You know how much you like partridge meat."

The fox nodded. "Yes, I am most fond of the bird— especially if it's in my stomach—but this time I have something more important on my mind than food. I *must* learn to whistle."

Without another word, the fox left the puma and went off in search of the partridge.

As the fox stalked the woods, the partridge saw him coming through the thicket and flew into a bush to hide. However, the fox saw her and called in the most gentle voice he could muster, "Don't be afraid, little partridge. I promise never to harm you or your family again if you will teach me to whistle as beautifully as you do."

Now the partridge was proud of her whistle and

pleased that anyone—even the fox—would want to imitate her. Nevertheless, she was cautious, remembering the many times he had tried to catch her.

"I'd gladly teach you, Mr. Fox, if I were sure you would keep your promise," said the foolish bird.

"Indeed I will," replied the fox. "Now let's begin the lesson at once."

The partridge flew several circles around the fox's head before she gained enough courage to land next to him. She peered at him closely for the first time.

"Well," she exclaimed, "no wonder you can't whistle! Your mouth is much too long. I'll have to sew it closed along each side to make it the right size for whistling."

"Sew up my mouth!" shouted the fox.

The bird flew back into the bush. She called in a quaking voice, "It will only hurt a very little."

"Come back then and do it!" commanded the fox, "for I must learn to whistle."

"Will you be patient and hold still?" she asked in a frightened voice.

"I'll do just as you say," answered the fox meekly.

Using a feather from her underwing for a needle, and a strong shoot of grass for thread, the partridge began to sew. She darned carefully with cross-stitches, making them small and tight. When only a ring-sized opening remained, she bit off the thread with her sharp beak and said, "Now I think your mouth is just right for whistling. Try it, Mr. Fox."

The fox released his breath. Such a fine, beautiful

whistle came forth that he leaped and danced for joy.

"Good! Good!" cried the partridge happily. "Soon you will be able to whistle as well as I do!"

"I can do that already," mumbled the fox through his clenched teeth, for he was unable to speak very well with such a small mouth. And he continued his whistling.

The partridge was dismayed by the fox's vanity and hurt by his ingratitude. "If you are doing so well by yourself," she said bravely, "you no longer need me around." And she started to fly away.

Immediately the fox forgot his promise. All he could see was a bird on the wing. Without thinking, he grabbed for the partridge with his mouth. Rip-rip-rip went all the stitches. Not a single one remained.

The partridge escaped unhurt, but not so the fox. His mouth was sore and bleeding. Worse yet, his hope of learning to whistle was gone forever.

He crept back to his den and lay in a dark corner. All he could think about was his puffy lips and empty stomach. He was miserable.

He covered his mouth with his large bushy tail and heaved a mournful sigh through his nose.

Never again did the fox try to whistle, and never again did a partridge go close to a fox.

The Lazy Fox

A TALE TOLD IN ARGENTINA

There was once a fox who was known throughout the land for being a lazy scamp as well as a scheming rascal. He was too lazy to work on his own little farm, and he was so scheming nobody would work for him. The fox was as full of tricks as a fig is of seeds.

One morning he looked at his barren fields and sighed, "Unless my fields are planted, I shall go hungry. But what can I do?"

He sat on his haunches and thought and thought. Finally, an idea popped into his head.

"I'll get that slow, stupid armadillo to plant my fields for me and I'll promise him a share of the crops. Of course," the fox added slyly, "it will be a very *small* share."

So the fox hurried down the path to the home of his neighbor. He found him sitting under a *quebracho* tree, telling stories to his children.

"Good day, friend armadillo," the fox called. "I have been thinking about you this morning, and I want to help you."

"Help me?" asked the armadillo, not able to believe his ears.

"Yes, indeed. Your ground is rocky and poor. Why don't you plant on my good land? I will ask only a small share of the crop as payment."

"That is very generous of you," the armadillo replied.

Now the armadillo knew he was no match for the cunning fox, and suspected a trick, but he did want to grow food on that rich soil.

"You may choose whatever you want to plant," urged the fox, "and I will take only half of it."

"That is fair enough," said the armadillo slowly.

"Better yet," suggested the fox, swishing his bushy tail, "I'll take only the part of the crop that grows beneath the soil. You may have all that grows above the ground."

"That is more than fair," the armadillo agreed.

Early the next morning, the armadillo and his family got busy in the fields. By the time the fox sauntered past, they were well along with their work. The fox was pleased to see how well his scheme was working, but he never bothered to ask what crop was being planted.

Raindrops fell on the dark, thirsty earth. Warm fingers of the sun reached down to the fields, caressing the new plants. How they grew! At last it was time to harvest the crop.

The armadillo brought his entire family to help him. And what a fine field of wheat they harvested! By the time the lazy fox went out to get his share, all that remained were the tasteless roots.

He was not only very angry, but he was very hungry, too. Hurrying over to the farm of the armadillo, he found him resting under his favorite tree, looking sleek and contented.

"You made a terrible blunder," the fox shouted at his neighbor. "I cannot eat roots! Surely you know that the good part of the wheat grows above the ground. But I forgive you. Next season we will work together again. Then what is below the soil will be yours, and I shall take what grows above."

"It seems a fair bargain," the armadillo said. "Do you want to choose the crop?"

"No, but you must choose it wisely. Just let me know when the food is ready to eat."

The next season the armadillo planted potatoes. Again the crop was large, but the fox could not eat the tops, which were above ground and lay withering in the sun.

He went to the farm of his neighbor. "Last season I thought you made a stupid mistake. But now I believe you are tricking me. I cannot eat the vines of the potato plants."

The armadillo squirmed in his suit of armor, and remained silent.

"I have made a great sacrifice to help you," the fox continued, "but you never think of me when you plant your crop. See how thin and weak I am."

"It is true that you are thin, but your coat fits you much better that way."

The fox glared at him. "We are going to try another plan. Next season, I shall take the tops of the plants as well as what grows beneath the soil. You may take what grows in the middle of the plants."

The armadillo remained silent.

"It is only right," added the fox, "that I have a larger share next year, because I have had nothing of the first two crops."

At last the armadillo replied, "Well, it seems a fair enough bargain." And he agreed.

The fox went happily up the path, sure that he could not be tricked again.

When planting time came again, the armadillo planted corn. The crop was large, with ears full and tender, but they grew in the middle of the stalk. There was nothing left for the fox but roots and husks.

The armadillo and his family were munching on the tempting ears of corn when they saw the fox running down the path toward them. His bushy tail trailed straight out behind him.

"You are just in time for a feast," greeted the armadillo. "Sit down and have a roasted ear and we shall talk of next season's crop."

"We shall not! For three seasons, you have tricked me."

The armadillo blinked his heavy eyelids. "I am sorry, but I gave you the part of the crop you asked for."

The fox looked hungrily at the corn, but he didn't sit down with his neighbors. Instead, he stared at the

"You are just in time for a feast," said the armadillo

armadillo, wondering why he had ever been stupid
enough to call *him* stupid!

"Next year I shall plant my crop, and keep all of it."
With that the fox went back up the path, his tail dragging
in the dust.

The armadillo reached for another ear of corn, and
seated himself under the *quebracho* tree. He was laughing
so merrily that he had to hang on to his bony armor to
keep it from cracking.

The Strange *Adventures* of *Alcavilu*

A TALE TOLD BY THE ARAUCANIAN INDIANS OF CHILE

One of the most interesting stories about the Araucanian Indians is the one that tells how their chieftains were named. The Araucanian men had to compete for this title by holding a heavy log on their shoulders. Tribal history tells of Caupolican, one young brave, who broke the record by holding a log aloft for three days. The Araucanian Indians enjoyed all sorts of contests. One of the most unusual was that of silence. Although fond of talking, the Indians would sit for days without speaking, hoping to win the contest. More than 100,000 descendants of these hardy people live in Chile. Many are skilled craftsmen and weavers; others are industrious farmers and excellent horsemen. The Araucanians are known for their courage, vigor, and patriotism.

Alcavilu, the handsome son of a chieftain, was a noble youth, kind-hearted and wise in the ways of his people.

One day Alcavilu said to his father, "I long to see what lies beyond the great mountains. Give me your blessing, for I wish to journey forth while the spring is here with its flowers and soft breezes."

The chieftain was sad to see his son go, but he gave

him his blessing, a fine horse with silver trappings, a deer-skin sack filled with food for the journey, and some magic leaves to ward off sickness and evil spirits.

It was with a light heart that young Alcavilu mounted his horse, waved farewell to his father, and set forth on his journey.

Through the wide valleys he rode, crossing little streams and flowery meadows where bees hummed at their work. The sun god was shining brightly overhead when he dismounted in a deep forest. He sat down to rest and eat his meal.

"Good day," said a voice near him.

Startled, Alcavilu turned quickly to see who, besides himself, was in such a lonely place. There stood an aged man, dressed in such ragged garments that he shivered from the cold.

"Good day," Alcavilu replied. He rose and went to the old man's side. "Come eat with me, grandfather, and let me give you my warm blanket."

Glad to be wrapped in the blanket, the old man sat down and shared Alcavilu's food with him. After he had finished eating, the aged one sat quietly for a long time. Finally, he spoke.

"I have looked into your future, my good youth, and I see you will have many strange adventures. And when you return home, you will not be alone."

"Thank you, grandfather, for telling me of my future," Alcavilu said.

The old man stood up. "Now I must leave, for I have far to travel, and my strength is failing. Accept this little

"I have looked into your future, my good youth

gift as a reward for sharing your food!" He gave Alcavilu
a small green leaf. "It is magic. Chew it, and you will be
able to understand the language of the birds and animals."

"How kind you are!" the chieftain's son answered, as
he took the leaf.

At that moment, a fox trotted through the nearby
trees, and Alcavilu cried out happily, "Look, grandfather,
it crossed our path from left to right. That means good
luck. Good luck for both of us!"

The aged one nodded, and started to move on.

"You must not travel on foot, grandfather. Take my
horse. He will take you safely to your journey's end. I am
strong, and can walk easier than you. And keep the
blanket, for the wind blows cold."

With many thanks, the old man wrapped himself in

and I see you will have many strange adventures"

the blanket, mounted the horse with the silver trappings, and rode through the forest. Alcavilu watched horse and rider until they disappeared from sight. Then, chewing the magic leaf, he set forth on foot.

The first night Alcavilu slept in the topmost branches of a tall tree, out of reach of wild animals. As the sky turned from gray to rose, he awakened to the chattering of birds around him. He heard the voices of animals beneath the tree. He listened.

True to the old man's words, he understood what they were saying.

"Good morning," he called to them in a language he had never spoken before. "Can you understand me?"

"Yes, yes," they answered. "Come down and talk with us!"

He climbed down, eager to find out what they would say to him.

The lion said, "Yesterday, an old man riding a fine horse with silver trappings told us to guard you while you slept, and we did so."

"Thank you, good friend," Alcavilu said.

"Before we leave you, we want you to accept this help for your journey." The lion pulled a pure white hair from his chest. He gave it to Alcavilu. "It is a magic hair. Keep it with you always, and you will have the power to change yourself into a bird or an animal, and go any place you wish."

"What the old man said is true," thought Alcavilu. "What strange adventures I am having!"

He thanked the lion for his gift. Then, holding the pure white hair in his hand, Alcavilu closed his eyes tightly, and wished to fly some place he had never been!

At once he was soaring up, up, up through the clouds. Hardly had he become used to flying when he felt himself coming back to earth. He landed at the edge of a great volcano, and became himself again.

"What are you doing here?" shouted a harsh voice.

Alcavilu looked around in wonderment. There was a cabin, and in its doorway stood a young girl. She looked frightened and pale. Surely, he thought, she was not the one who had shouted to him! He took a step toward her, and then saw a fierce-looking young man.

Before Alcavilu could reply, loud roars and great puffs of steam began coming from the volcano.

Alcavilu found himself nestled between two soft hands

"Run for your life," cried the young man. "Here comes Cherufe, god of the volcano. If he finds you here he will throw you into the fiery crater."

"Who are you?" asked Alcavilu, thinking the young man might want only to be rid of him.

"I am his servant. I know his ways."

Once more Alcavilu turned himself into a bird and flew away. He meant to seek the home of some kind person who would give him food and shelter for the night.

Alcavilu flew on until he found a sturdy plant growing by the door of a neat cottage. He perched on a stem of the plant, and decided to rest before he changed himself back into the son of the chieftain.

He was so tired that, before he knew it, he was asleep. He was awakened by a sweet voice that said, "Look, father, at the little bird I have caught."

Alcavilu opened his eyes. He found himself nestled between two soft hands. He looked up, and saw the prettiest face he had ever seen. It was that of a young girl.

"Put him in this cage, and hang it in the kitchen, Kallfuray," said the father. "He will be company for you while your brothers and I work in the fields."

From his cage Alcavilu watched Kallfuray as she went about her household tasks. She stopped often, coming to him, and putting her lips up to the cage. Each time she stopped, she told her new pet, "I love you."

Kallfuray began to sing, and her voice was as sweet as Alcavilu had believed it to be. She sang:

If I had a crown of moonbeams,
Or a crown of the sun's bright rays,

I'd wed a noble chieftain's son,
And live happily all my days.

Alcavilu wanted to chuckle at the words of her song, but, being a bird, he could only chirp merrily. When the family seated itself for supper, how he wished that he might sit with them, enjoying the food that smelled so good. Instead, he picked at the bird seed, which had been put in his cage by the thoughtful Kallfuray.

By the time the little home was in darkness, and each member of the family was asleep, poor Alcavilu was so hungry he could scarcely endure it. Then he had an idea. "Why don't I change myself into something small enough to get out of the cage, crawl to the cupboard, and change myself into Alcavilu again? Then I can eat food that I have seen Kallfuray put there."

Alcavilu used his magic hair and changed himself into an ant. He crawled out of the cage, down a wall, and onto the floor of the kitchen. There, he became himself once more.

He had just started to chew on a piece of juicy meat when he heard Kallfuray say, "Father, someone is in the kitchen."

A moment later, Alcavilu found all the family around him. "What is the meaning of this?" they shouted. "Where did you come from?"

Alcavilu told them of his strange adventures and, when he described the girl near the volcano, the father cried out, "That is my other daughter! My dear Murtilla! Many moons ago, the volcano stole her, and we have never been able to find her."

"I'll go now and bring her home to you," said Al-cavilu.

"It will be a dangerous mission," replied the father. "Let Kallfuray prepare a meal for you before you leave."

But Alcavilu politely refused, for he was eager to be on his way. So, changing into a bird, he flew to the volcano. There, outside the cabin door stood Murtilla, the sister of gentle Kallfuray.

Inside he could hear the loud snores of Cherufe, the god of the volcano. His servant was also asleep.

Alcavilu whispered to the surprised Murtilla, telling her why he was there, and how he came to be in the form of a bird. "As soon as I change into a lion, get on my back, and hold tightly to my mane," he said.

Without a word, Murtilla did as she was told.

When Alcavilu reached the cottage with Murtilla, there was great rejoicing. Kallfuray kissed her sister and the two cried with happiness. The others gathered around, talking and laughing.

The grateful father said to Alcavilu, "I wish we could give you a gift worthy of your deed, dear friend, but that is impossible because we are poor."

"There is only one gift I long to have and that is Kallfuray's hand in marriage. I love her with all my heart," replied Alcavilu.

Kallfuray, blushing happily, came to her father's side. "Even when he was a bird, I loved him, and he will always have my love."

At that moment, a horse was heard neighing in

front of the cottage. The aged man of the forest stood in the doorway.

"Good day, Alcavilu. I am returning your blanket and your horse which you so unselfishly gave me. In the saddle bags you will find gold and precious stones for you and your bride."

"Thank you, grandfather, for your gifts. You spoke truly when we met in the forest. I have had many strange adventures and I am not returning home alone. Kallfuray is going with me and she will become my bride."

The aged man smiled wisely. Then he disappeared.

Alcavilu set Kallfuray on his horse. They waved farewell to her family, and were gone.

The chieftain greeted his son with open arms and gazed at Kallfuray with approval. Then, what a great wedding he gave them!

Many, many years later, when the chieftain died, Alcavilu took his place. He was a wise and kind ruler, and a very happy one, with lovely Kallfuray at his side.

The Gift of the Moon Goddess

A TALE TOLD BY THE GUARANI INDIANS OF PARAGUAY

At one time, the homes of the Guarani Indians were scattered throughout central and southern Brazil, eastern Bolivia, Uruguay, and northeastern Argentina. They now reside mainly in Paraguay. Guarani means warrior and, before the sixteenth century, the wandering tribes were fierce and warlike. However, since the arrival of the white man and Christianity, the Guarani population has become peace-loving and industrious. A favorite tea of the ancient Guarani, made of the yerba maté, is an important product of Paraguay. Another export, calling for the remarkable skill and patience of the Indian women, is their world-famous lace. Although Spanish is the official language of Paraguay, Gaurani is spoken by most of the people living in both the rural and urban communities. Paraguay is the only American nation that has an Indian tongue as the "popular" language.

Yerba maté, a tea used in South America, tastes a little like the green tea of the United States. However, it is so nutritious that it is sometimes called a "liquid vegetable."

Often yerba maté and meat were the daily fare of the gaucho—the South American cowboy—for many weeks at a time. Yet he lived a long and active life caring for the great herds that roamed the pampas—large, tree-less plains, like those of our Middle West.

The Guarani Indians of Argentina and Paraguay tell how yerba maté came into the world. This story is very old. It goes back to the time when the gods and goddesses left the heavens and came down to visit the earth.

One of these heavenly visitors was the Moon Goddess. She loved to pick the flowers in the land of the Guaranis. She was a frequent visitor, but came only during the day. At night she had to be in the sky, ready to cast her silver light over the sleeping land.

Her companion was a Cloud Goddess. Each took the form and manner of dress of a Guarani maiden so they might wander through field and forest, and no one would know they were goddesses.

One springtime afternoon, they were so happy picking flowers that time passed too quickly. They were not aware that night was near until long, dark shadows fell across the meadow.

"We must go at once," cried the Moon Goddess.

"Just a minute longer," begged the Cloud Goddess. "I see some white orchids growing in the forest, and I want to pick a bouquet."

"There is not much time left," the Moon Goddess reminded her, worried at any delay.

They walked quickly into the forest to reach the orchids. Then they cried out in terror. In their path crouched a tiger, the largest they had ever seen. His eyes glared. His great mouth hung open. The Moon and Cloud

The tiger leaped once more . . . The Indian aimed an

goddesses clung to each other. They were so frightened they forgot to change themselves into their heavenly forms.

The tiger leaped at them with a roar, but in mid-air a whistling arrow pierced his side. He fell to the ground, howling in rage.

An aged Guarani Indian darted from behind a tree. "Run!" he cried to the goddesses. "Run for your lives."

But they were as rooted to the earth as the trees around them.

The tiger sprang to his feet, and leaped once more at the goddesses. At that moment the Indian aimed an arrow at the beast's heart, and this time the arrow hit its mark. The tiger lay mortally wounded at their feet.

When the Moon and Cloud goddesses realized they

arrow at the beast's heart, and this time the arrow hit

were out of danger, they transformed themselves, and rose to the sky.

"He is dead," said the Indian. He looked up to tell the maidens. There was no trace of them. He searched the forest, but they were not to be found.

Finally, he convinced himself that he had dreamed the whole thing.

But when he came back from his search, there lay the tiger, and also, on the ground, were the flowers the maidens had been carrying. He knew then that he had not been dreaming.

Night had, by that time, drawn its great curtain of blackness across the earth, so the Indian climbed into a tall tree where he slept. In his dreams, the maidens came to him. Each told her name, and thanked him for saving her life. The Cloud Goddess then disappeared, but the Moon Goddess stayed to talk.

The Moon Goddess, known to the Guaranis as the Protectress of Good People, said to him, "Because of your good deed, I shall give you and your people a valuable tree. From the toasted leaves you can make a tea that will serve as food for the hungry. It will refresh all who drink it. You will find this tree growing at the very spot where I stood."

"What a strange dream," the old man said when he awoke. He climbed down from his shelter, and walked to the place where the Moon Goddess had been attacked by the tiger.

Just as the goddess foretold, there grew a beautiful tree, its leaves dark green and shining.

He took some of the leaves from the tree back to his village, and told his tribe about his adventure and reward. They toasted the leaves over a tribal fire, and made the tea. It satisfied their hunger, and refreshed them, just as the Moon Goddess had promised.

That evening the villagers knelt down on the ground, their faces lifted to the sky, and thanked the Moon Goddess for her wonderful gift of yerba maté.

The White Spider's Gift

A TALE TOLD BY THE GUARANI INDIANS OF PARAGUAY

In distant Paraguay, at the edge of a dense forest, lived a widow and her only son. His name was Pikí.

One morning—as was their daily habit—Pikí and his mother went to fill their large earthen jars with water. On the way to the cool, bubbling spring, Pikí paused to look at a yerba maté bush. He called out to his mother, "Look, Mother, my little white spider is waiting to greet me!"

Pikí knelt by the bush. His mother joined him. Kneeling beside Pikí, she smiled at his unusual friend. She well remembered the day, long ago, when Pikí told how he had rescued the tiny white spider from drowning in the spring where it had fallen. When it had first been pulled out of the water, the spider had nestled, exhausted, in Pikí's hand. Then, as if to express its thanks, it had danced about on all its merry legs.

But now, kneeling beside the bush on which the tiny white spider rested, Pikí was no longer that small child. He was a strong, handsome lad of eighteen. The spider crawled from the bush onto Pikí's finger and then into his palm. The young man's mother felt a great tenderness come over her as she watched her gentle son.

At that moment there was a splash of oars. Pikí and his mother looked up and saw a beautiful Indian maiden paddling her canoe down the stream. Her white cotton tunic was gathered at the waist by a wide purple sash. Her shining black braids were entwined with matching flowers. Her large dark eyes, warm and friendly, sparkled like the sunbeams on the water.

It was not until she was out of sight that Pikí turned to his mother and exclaimed, "Isn't she beautiful! Who is she?"

"Return your friend spider to the bush for we must get our jars of water. On our way home I will tell you about the maiden. But we must hurry, for we have corn to grind and meat that must be dried before the sun goes down."

Pikí did his mother's bidding. As they walked along the forest path, carrying the jars on their shoulders, his mother said, "Her name is Tukira. She is the chieftain's daughter."

The youth was surprised. "But how strange that I have never seen her before in the village!"

"She has only just returned," his mother answered. "Since her mother's death, Tukira has lived with an aunt in a distant village."

"Will she now stay with our people?" Pikí asked hopefully.

"Yes," his mother said, smiling. "The time has come

for her to marry. As is our custom, the chieftain will choose the right husband for Tukira."

It happened a few days later—when Pikí was in the forest gathering berries—that he saw Tukira picking fresh flowers for her hair. Startled, the Indian princess looked up at him. Pikí offered her some of the luscious fruit from his basket. Soon they were both happily engaged in conversation and laughter.

The next day the pair met in the same way. Soon they were planning such meetings. By the beginning of summer, the whole tribe—including the chieftain—knew that Tukira and Pikí loved each other.

However, the chieftain wished to give the princes of other tribes, and his own brave warriors, an opportunity to compete for his daughter's hand.

Messengers were sent far and wide announcing contests that would be held during the next month. When the day arrived for the competition to begin, many warriors and handsome princes assembled in the village. What fine and noble youths they were!

But Pikí held his own with them and won his share of the events.

On the final day of competition, the chieftain startled everyone by saying, "There will be no further contests of racing, swimming, or hunting. Instead, all the valiant youths, who have won in the various competitions, will have to prove themselves in another way. The one who presents my daughter with the most exquisite and original gift shall win her hand in marriage. I give each of you two moons in which to find such a gift."

This was very discouraging to Pikí, for he was a poor lad and knew nothing of treasures from faraway places. His days had been spent doing useful but humble tasks for his mother.

Tukira tried to comfort him. "Do not despair," she said. "Ask god Tupá for help. He always rewards good people."

Pikí prayed to Tupá. But no answer came.

Before long, many of the other youths brought their rare and beautiful gifts. There were skins of strange animals fashioned into rugs and wall hangings. Large plumes and many shades of feathers were woven into fancy headdresses. Jewelry of rare metals was encrusted with precious stones. Unusual songbirds were brought in gilded cages. One of these was even able to speak a few words of greeting.

Upon seeing these things, Pikí turned his back and sadly returned to his home. His mother tried to console him, but he shook his head.

"I have failed," he told her. "I can never win Tukira for my bride. I am going to the stream where I first saw her and shall remain until after the wedding festivities are over."

When he reached the spring, he heard a gentle voice from the yerba maté shrub. "Pikí," it called to him, "I am here in the bush. I am your little white spider, and I shall help you win the hand of your princess."

"Dear little friend," Pikí cried in surprise, "I didn't know you could talk!"

"The gift of speech comes from god Tupá. He has asked me to help you."

"But how?" asked the youth.

"Go home to your mother and cheer her, for she is very sad. Return tomorrow at sunrise. Your special gift for Tukira will be ready."

Pikí ran all the way home and joyfully shared this news with his mother.

Meanwhile, the small white spider worked throughout the night weaving delicate threads that glistened in the moonlight. The center of the web was patterned after the guava flower. As the web increased in size, designs of birds, orchids, begonias, and other flowers appeared in it. The web became a glorious mantle of shimmering lace.

When the sun tinted the eastern sky, Pikí awoke and hurried toward the spider's home. There at the bottom of the yerba maté bush lay the marvelous lace mantle. How fine and strong were the silken threads! How beautiful the design! Pikí knew at once that none of the other gifts presented to Tukira could compare with this treasure.

"Take it to the one who will be your bride, but hurry or you will be late!" urged the friendly spider.

"Thank you with all my heart," said Pikí as he carefully folded the mantle. "But first I shall show it to my mother. Then we shall hasten to the village."

Pikí and his mother arrived just in time. The chief-

Piki gently placed the lace mantle over Tukira's head

tain stood with Tukira by his side. He was ready to announce who her bridegroom would be.

Pikí rushed forward and gently placed the precious lace mantle over Tukira's head and shoulders. She exclaimed at its loveliness and put out her hand to Pikí. The crowd gasped in surprise. Even the chieftain looked amazed and pleased.

"Pikí has won!" proclaimed the chieftain.

And the people shouted in agreement, "Pikí has won! His gift is the most beautiful!"

That very day Pikí and Tukira were married amidst great rejoicing. The lace mantle was worn as a veil and everyone agreed there had never been a bride more beautiful.

While the drums sounded and the warriors chanted, Pikí gave thanks to Tupá and the little white spider. His mother, too, sang praises and gave thanks for her son's good fortune.

As for Tukira, she was so happy she never thought to question where the wonderful gift came from or who had woven the intricate patterns.

Many women of the village tried to weave the same beautiful lace on their looms. Although some succeeded in creating fancy lace mantles, none were as finely woven as the little white spider's.

If you were to visit Paraguay today, you would still see women of the villages making *ñandutí*, or spider's-web, lace—famous throughout the world for its delicate beauty.

The Great White Condor

A TALE TOLD BY THE AYMARAN INDIANS OF BOLIVIA

The Aymaran Indians of today are a mixture of all the ancient races that roamed the highlands of Peru and Bolivia, but they are justly proud of their Aymaran heritage. It is reported by historians that their civilization preceded that of the Incas and, in some respects, was more highly developed. This is substantiated by the marvellous figures and intricately carved monuments that have been found and have been attributed to this tribe. Although the Aymaras were forced to become a part of the Inca Empire and, later, a part of the Spanish colony, they refused to adopt a language other than their own. Even today, they maintain their individual manner of dress, customs, and religion. Their method of farming, also, has changed little over the centuries.

When the world was still new, the gods divided the land among the many Indian tribes. To their favorite people, the Sapallas, they gave the choicest spot, a beautiful and rich valley encircled by snow-capped mountains. The Sapallas proved themselves worthy of this gift by living a good, industrious life, as commanded by their gods.

Time passed, and the Sapallas knew only peace and happiness in their sheltered homeland.

Meanwhile, on the other side of the mountain range —lands belonging to a warlike tribe called the Karis—a volcano had erupted and covered the surrounding lands with lava and ashes. Having to search for a new home, the Karis crossed over the mighty mountains and swept through the valley of the Sapallas like a swarm of hungry locusts. They imprisoned the Sapalla chieftain and the wise men, and took possession of all the land, houses, and flocks. They made slaves of the Sapalla Indians, forcing them to eat the poorest food and seek shelter with the animals.

Before the chieftain was led away to prison, he was granted permission to speak to Choque, his only son. "Although you are only a child, you must take my place," he said. "Be an example of courage. Tell our people that the gods will never forsake them."

"I shall do what you ask, Father," the lad said, trying to hide his tears.

Of course the Karis never considered young Choque as a threat. In their eyes he was only a harmless boy.

Each day the Sapallas suffered more and more under the cruel hand of the Karis. The poor victims soon began to lose faith in their gods—all, that is, except young Choque, who remembered his father's words.

Every afternoon Choque would trudge up the mountain to pray to the gods for help.

When he returned he would find his people gathered

"You must take my place," his father said

together mourning. "Surely our gods have forsaken us," they said. "We shall never be free again."

Young Choque tried to comfort them. "Although our days are wearisome, we must never lose faith. I know that the gods are still with us."

"If that is true, why must we suffer?"

Choque could only shake his head sadly and add, "My heart tells me that the gods who gave us this valley will help us if we will trust them."

One afternoon, as Choque was coming down from

the mountain, a great white condor flew in front of him.

At once Choque took out his sling.

"Put it away and have no fear," said the bird, lighting on a rock nearby.

Choque returned the sling to his belt. "Who are you? Why do you come to me?"

"I am the great god Pachacámac. I have taken the form of a condor to bring you a message from all the gods who are pleased with your faith and courage, Choque."

Choque was very humble. "Oh, noble god, what is the message?"

"Tonight, bring your people here in secret. On this spot you will find a large quantity of seeds of a kind never before seen by man."

"And what shall we do with them, kind god?"

"Tomorrow you and your people will plant this seed in the furrows, instead of the seed given you by the Karis. When harvest time comes, you will understand. Do you promise to do your part?"

"Oh yes," said young Choque, "I promise."

The white condor stretched his enormous wings and soared back into the clouds.

The Sapallas obeyed young Choque and planted the seeds carefully.

Each day the sun god gave out more heat and the plants began to sprout in the neat furrows. Before long, small green balls appeared at the ends of the vines.

Although Choque was very busy helping to tend the plants, he still took time to go to the mountain to pray.

One afternoon the white condor visited him again.

"Put the sling away and have no fear," said the bird

"Harvest time is not far off," the condor said. "The Karis are eager and curious to eat the fruit of this new plant."

Choque nodded. "They say it is a gift from their gods."

"Obey their orders to pick all the green balls growing at the ends of the vines, but warn your people not to eat these. They must not even taste one of them."

Choque was disappointed. "But I thought the gods were giving us, the Sapallas, this plant."

"The false crop is above the ground. That is for the Karis. Beneath the soil lies the good, nourishing food for the Sapallas. When the vines wither, take your people in secret and gather this crop."

Choque was ashamed that he had ever doubted the condor. With bowed head he exclaimed, "You and the other gods are so kind to us! Is there something more we should do?"

The great white condor advised the lad, "Gather many rocks for your slings and store them carefully. When I give the signal, use them against the Karis."

"With the help of the gods we can do this," Choque replied humbly.

So it was that the green balls were picked and stored away for the Karis to eat at a gay fiesta that they were planning. Following Choque's instructions, the Sapallas did not taste the green balls, but hurried away to gather rocks for their slings.

Later, in the dark of the night, the Sapallas crept

along the ground, harvesting the crop beneath the soil. This they concealed along with their rocks.

For the third time the white condor appeared and spoke to Choque. "Tomorrow the Karis celebrate their fiesta. They will eat their new food for the first time. It is on this day that you will drive them from your land with your sling shots."

Young Choque's faith had never been stronger. When he returned to his people, he told them what the white condor had said.

Early the following morning, the Karis gathered and, after singing and dancing, they began to feast on the green balls of the new plant. But soon many grew dizzy and faint.

"We have been poisoned," they moaned as they stumbled and fell over each other.

Choque knew the time was ripe for attack. He beckoned to the waiting Sapallas, who drove the weakened Karis back across the mountains.

Soon Choque's father, the chieftain, and the wise men were released from their prison, and once more peace and happiness reigned among the Sapallas.

And what of this new plant that the white condor had given to brave young Choque and his people? It continued to thrive in the valley and was known as the potato.

The Little Frog of the Stream

A TALE TOLD IN PERU

In a cool, clear stream there lived a kind little frog who believed that her face was quite ugly. Every day she looked at her brothers and sisters and thought, "How beautiful they are! If only I could look like them!"

At one side of the stream rose a mountain so high that its snowy peak was hidden among the clouds. It was on the side of this mountain that the condor, king of birds, found a great rocky ledge on which to build his home. It was a fine home! The silky skins of vicuñas—the natural prey of King Condor—covered the walls and floors. The great bird's bed was of soft feathers. His pantry was stocked with choice meats.

Unlike human kings, the condor had only one servant. She was a poor little shepherdess whom he had carried off one day while she drove her flock of llamas to pasture. The shepherdess's name was Collyur, which means "Morning Star." This name had been given her by her parents because they thought she was as beautiful as their favorite star.

The frog often watched Collyur standing in the doorway of the bird's home, when the condor was absent, and saw the shepherdess looking sorrowfully into the distance.

One morning, after the condor had taken his nap, Collyur asked him, "May I go down to the stream to wash my clothes?"

"No, indeed," said the condor, scowling. "You stay here, and prepare my dinner."

"It's all prepared, sir. Therefore, please let me go."

The condor looked at her sharply. "If I let you go alone, you will try to escape!"

The child swallowed hard, and thought quickly. She answered, "Of course I will not. Besides, as long as you hear me beat my clothes on the rocks to get them clean, you will know I have not run away."

"Very well, then, you may go. But if you try to escape, I shall punish you severely."

So Collyur, carrying her little bundle of clothes on her head, made her way down to the stream. On reaching the shore, she knelt on the rocks and soaked her clothes in the water. Then she began to beat them on the rocks, crying bitterly all the while.

Suddenly, she heard a voice say, "Dear child, do not despair. I shall help you."

Collyur looked around and saw the little frog perched on the rock at her side. She did not think the frog's face was ugly. To her, it had kind eyes and a sympathetic voice which comforted her.

"Oh, please help me, little frog! I am so miserable!" said Collyur, beginning to weep again.

"Dear child, do not despair. I shall help you"

"Now, please don't cry or I can't help you. Just dry your eyes and listen."

"Yes, I'll dry my tears, dear little frog."

"I was born with a magic power which allows me to take the shape of anyone I wish to help. In a moment, I shall take on your appearance, and begin beating the clothes on the rocks. As long as the condor hears that sound, he will not be suspicious. When I begin beating the clothes, you must run quickly. Go to the house by the edge of the woods where a good shepherd and his wife live. They will help you find your way home."

"Thank you with all my heart," the child said, as she bent over to kiss the little frog on the forehead.

As soon as the frog changed into a little girl who was the image of Collyur, the real Collyur ran as fast as she could toward the shepherd's home. All the way she could hear the frog-child as she beat, beat, beat the clothes.

"What is keeping that lazy child?" asked the condor of himself as he finished his tasty meal of vicuña. "If she doesn't stop beating her clothes, they will be in rags and tatters. I will fly down to the stream and scold her."

The loud whir of the condor's wings warned the frog-child of the condor's approach.

"Stop that beating and go back to the house," shouted the condor from the great rock where he perched.

He was utterly surprised when the child stood up, stepped into the stream, and disappeared beneath the water. There she became a frog again.

"Come back here," shrieked the condor. He flew down and looked into the stream. All he saw was his own reflection in the calm, clear water. Puzzled, he flew back home in a rage.

Meanwhile, the frog returned upstream to her sisters and brothers. But something strange had happened to her. She knew this because of the surprised look on the faces of the other frogs and the fish who crowded around her.

"What is it?" asked the little frog.

"It is your forehead!" the frogs exclaimed. "There is a beautiful star-shaped jewel on it!"

A lovely jewel shone on the spot where Collyur had bestowed a kiss. It was like the morning star!

The frogs hopped excitedly. The fish, eager to rejoice with them, made a circle, their glistening fins touching, and swam around the little frog singing:

Glug, glug,
You are beautiful now,
With a shining jewel
Upon your brow.

Then, with their fat little hands clasped, the proud frogs hopped about the little frog, and said:

Croak, croak,
To show how kind
And good you are,
On your forehead
Was left a star.

From that day on, the little frog, who had always been loved for her kindness, was called the Queen of the Stream. And never again was she troubled about her looks.

The Fox and the Mole

A TALE TOLD IN PERU

Once a fox and a mole were neighbors. Each lived in his own snug little cave at the foot of a rocky hill. Although their ways were quite different, they got along together very happily.

The fox was carefree, and spent his days roaming through the fields and forest in search of food and adventure. But the mole stayed close to home, and dug for worms that lay around the roots of plants growing near the caves.

One night, when the new moon cast a faint silver light over hill and fields, the fox visited the mole as he was sitting in front of his cave.

"What is your dearest wish, Mole?" asked the fox.

The mole answered promptly, "To have my pantry filled with those good worms that live around the potato roots. What do you wish for? Is it doves or partridges?"

"Nothing like that," the fox replied gaily. "I wish to get to the moon."

"To the moon?" the mole asked in astonishment, as if he did not hear correctly. "Did you say 'to the moon'?"

"Yes, to the moon. I would rather go there than travel to the sun or to the stars or roam the earth."

The mole shook his head in wonderment. "But how can you get there?"

" I wish I knew!" the fox said, with a deep sigh.

It was only a few days later, as the fox was tying a rope around a bundle of firewood, that a wonderful idea came to him. He shouted joyfully. "Now I know how to get to the moon! It's very simple. If I can get the condor to tie a rope to the tip of the moon, I can easily *climb* up there."

The fox picked up the firewood and rushed home. Excitedly, he called to the mole, "Good news! Come out and hear the good news!"

The mole appeared in his doorway. "What is it?"

"Tonight you and I are going to the moon. We will get the condor to help us!"

The mole hesitated for a moment, then inquired, "Will there be food for us on the moon?"

"Of course," the fox assured his neighbor.

"Then I will go," the mole answered.

"Wait here!" the fox commanded. He bounded toward the top of the hill, where the great condor lived.

"Good day, friend Condor," the fox called. "Will you help me?"

"Good day, Fox. Sit down, and tell me what you want me to do."

"Tonight Mole and I want to go to the moon, and you are the only one who can help us get there."

"I cannot carry you up there, because I am afraid to land on the moon."

"But would you be willing to fly near the moon?"

The condor nodded.

"Good!" said the fox. "Now I will get enough rope to reach the moon. Take one end of the rope in your strong beak, and fasten it securely to the tip of the new moon. Are you willing to do this?"

The condor agreed to the plan and said, "I shall begin my flight when I pick up the rope at your cave."

When darkness fell, the fox and the mole were impatiently waiting for the great bird. In front of the caves lay coils upon coils of strong rope made of the *cortadera* plant.

Finally, the condor arrived.

"All is ready," said the fox.

The condor took hold of the rope in his beak. As he flew, the rope rose up, up, up, higher and higher. The fox and the mole watched in awe. Finally, the condor returned from his long flight.

"The rope is tied securely," the condor reported. "But until you are on your way, I shall fly along with you."

The fox and the mole thanked the condor and made ready to start their climb.

The fox felt gay and fearless, but he knew Mole was nervous, so he said, "I shall go first so that I can warn you of any danger that may lie ahead."

"Good! But I am beginning to wonder if the food on the moon will be as good as it is here."

As the condor flew, the rope rose up higher and higher

"Don't worry. It will be much better," the fox assured him cheerfully, as he started to climb up the rope.

The climbing fox was followed by the climbing mole. Up they went, paw over paw, paw over paw. Soon they were high above the treetops! Then they were looking down on the hill where they lived.

All at once they heard a loud, screeching "Ha, ha, ha!" It was the voice of a bright-colored parrot with beautiful green wings. It circled around them.

Thinking that the parrot was mocking them, the mole became angry. He stopped climbing, and shouted, "Be quiet, you clumsy, chattering longbeak. You are jealous because you cannot go to the moon."

Instead of answering, the parrot circled around and around the mole, each time coming closer.

"Silly nitwit, go back to earth. You will never get to the moon," the mole shouted.

"Ha, ha, ha! Neither will you!" the parrot replied, laughing.

Then the parrot flew to the rope above the mole's head. He began to peck, peck, peck with his sharp beak.

"Stop, stop!" pleaded the mole. "If you stop pecking at the rope, I will give you enough corn to last a lifetime! White corn, yellow corn, purple corn, any color you wish!"

The parrot was too busy to answer.

"Peck, peck, peck." Then, CR-R-R-ACK, the rope broke.

The condor, flying beneath the mole, was prepared

for this terrible moment. He caught the mole on his back, and flew him safely to his cave.

When the animals heard how foolish the mole had been, they began to taunt him and all his relatives. To avoid hearing these unkind remarks, all the moles left their dwellings in caves and rocks. They made homes for themselves beneath the earth. Since then they have lived in those burrows and come out only at night when the other animals are asleep.

And what happened to the fox? In Peru, it is said that on clear nights the fox can be seen standing on the moon and looking down on the earth.

And when the new moon appears, a bit of rope can still be seen dangling from the tip, if one looks very, very closely.

The Search for the *Magic Lake*

A TALE TOLD BY THE INCA INDIANS OF ECUADOR

The Inca Empire was founded in the twelfth century, in the city of Cuzco, Peru. The people believed that the founder was directly related to the sun god. Within a century, the Incas controlled a vast and highly organized empire, occupying land almost twice the size of our own California. In Cuzco, the home of the emperors and the center of activity, the Incas built a city of great splendor. Many of the buildings were constructed of pure gold. It was this golden treasure that drew Francisco Pizarro to Peru. Soon after he arrived, he and his followers took over the land for the Spanish. About three million descendants of the Incas still live in Ecuador, Bolivia, and Peru.

Long ago there was a ruler of the vast Inca Empire who had an only son. This youth brought great joy to his father's heart but also a sadness, for the prince had been born in ill health.

As the years passed the prince's health did not improve, and none of the court doctors could find a cure for his illness.

One night the aged emperor went down on his knees and prayed at the altar.

"Oh Great Ones," he said, "I am getting older and will soon leave my people and join you in the heavens. There is no one to look after them but my son, the prince. I pray you make him well and strong so he can be a fit ruler for my people. Tell me how his malady can be cured."

The emperor put his head in his hands and waited for an answer. Soon he heard a voice coming from the fire that burned constantly in front of the altar.

"Let the prince drink water from the magic lake at the end of the world," the voice said, "and he will be well."

At that moment the fire sputtered and died. Among the cold ashes lay a golden flask.

But the emperor was much too old to make the long journey to the end of the world, and the young prince was too ill to travel. So the emperor proclaimed that whosoever should fill the golden flask with the magic water would be greatly rewarded.

Many brave men set out to search for the magic lake, but none could find it. Days and weeks passed and still the flask remained empty.

In a valley, some distance from the emperor's palace, lived a poor farmer who had a wife, two grown sons, and a young daughter.

One day the older son said to his father, "Let my

brother and me join in the search for the magic lake. Before the moon is new again, we shall return and help you harvest the corn and potatoes."

The father remained silent. He was not thinking of the harvest, but feared for his sons' safety.

When the father did not answer, the second son added, "Think of the rich reward, Father!"

"It is their duty to go," said his wife, "for we must all try to help our emperor and the young prince."

After his wife had spoken, the father yielded.

"Go if you must, but beware of the wild beasts and evil spirits," he cautioned.

With their parents' blessing, and an affectionate farewell from their young sister, the sons set out on their journey.

They found many lakes, but none where the sky touched the water.

Finally the younger brother said, "Before another day has passed we must return to help father with the harvest."

"Yes," agreed the other, "but I have thought of a plan. Let us each carry a jar of water from any lake along the way. We can say it will cure the prince. Even if it doesn't, surely the emperor will give us a small reward for our trouble."

"Agreed," said the younger brother.

On arriving at the palace, the deceitful youths told the emperor and his court that they brought water from the magic lake. At once the prince was given a sip from each of the brothers' jars, but of course he remained as ill as before.

"Perhaps the water must be sipped from the golden flask," one of the high priests said.

But the golden flask would not hold the water. In some mysterious way the water from the jars disappeared as soon as it was poured into the flask.

In despair the emperor called for his magician and said to him, "Can you break the spell of the flask so the water will remain for my son to drink?"

"I cannot do that, your majesty," replied the magician. "But I believe," he added wisely, "that the flask is telling us that we have been deceived by the two brothers. The flask can be filled only with water from the magic lake."

When the brothers heard this, they trembled with fright, for they knew their falsehood was discovered.

So angry was the emperor that he ordered the brothers thrown into chains. Each day they were forced to drink water from their jars as a reminder of their false deed. News of their disgrace spread far and wide.

Again the emperor sent messengers throughout the land pleading for someone to bring the magic water before death claimed him and the young prince.

Súmac, the little sister of the deceitful youths, was tending her flock of llamas when she heard the sound of the royal trumpet. Then came the voice of the emperor's servant with his urgent message from the court.

Quickly the child led her llamas home and begged

her parents to let her go in search of the magic water.

"You are too young," her father said. "Besides, look at what has already befallen your brothers. Some evil spirit must have taken hold of them to make them tell such a lie."

And her mother said, "We could not bear to be without our precious Súmac!"

"But think how sad our emperor will be if the young prince dies," replied the innocent child. "And if I can find the magic lake, perhaps the emperor will forgive my brothers and send them home."

"Dear husband," said Súmac's mother, "maybe it is the will of the gods that we let her go."

Once again the father gave his permission.

"It is true," he murmured, "I must think of our emperor."

Súmac was overjoyed, and went skipping out to the corral to harness one of her pet llamas. It would carry her provisions and keep her company.

Meanwhile her mother filled a little woven bag with food and drink for Súmac—toasted golden kernels of corn and a little earthen jar of *chicha,* a beverage made from crushed corn.

The three embraced each other tearfully before Súmac set out bravely on her mission, leading her pet llama along the trail.

The first night she slept, snug and warm against her llama, in the shelter of a few rocks. But when she heard the hungry cry of the puma, she feared for her pet animal and bade it return safely home.

The next night she spent in the top branches of a tall tree, far out of reach of the dreadful puma. She hid her provisions in a hole in the tree trunk.

At sunrise she was aroused by the voices of gentle sparrows resting on a nearby limb.

"Poor child," said the oldest sparrow, "she can never find her way to the lake."

"Let us help her," chorused the others.

"Oh please do!" implored the child, "and forgive me for intruding in your tree."

"We welcome you," chirped another sparrow, "for you are the same little girl who yesterday shared your golden corn with us."

"We shall help you," continued the first sparrow, who was the leader, "for you are a good child. Each of us will give you a wing feather, and you must hold them all together in one hand as a fan. The feathers have magic powers that will carry you wherever you wish to go. They will also protect you from harm."

Each sparrow then lifted a wing, sought out a special feather hidden underneath, and gave it to Súmac. She fashioned them into the shape of a little fan, taking the ribbon from her hair to bind the feathers together so none would be lost.

"I must warn you," said the oldest sparrow, "that the lake is guarded by three terrible creatures. But have no fear. Hold the magic fan up to your face and you will be unharmed."

Súmac thanked the birds over and over again. Then, holding up the fan in her chubby hands, she said politely,

"We shall help you ... Each of us will give you a feather ..."

"Please, magic fan, take me to the lake at the end of the world."

A soft breeze swept her out of the top branches of the tree and through the valley. Then up she was carried, higher and higher into the sky, until she could look down and see the great mountain peaks covered with snow.

At last the wind put her down on the shore of a beautiful lake. It was, indeed, the lake at the end of the world, for, on the opposite side from where she stood, the sky came down so low it touched the water.

Súmac tucked the magic fan into her waistband and ran to the edge of the water. Suddenly her face fell. She had left everything back in the forest. What could she use for carrying the precious water back to the prince?

"Oh, I do wish I had remembered the jar!" she said, weeping.

Suddenly she heard a soft thud in the sand at her feet. She looked down and discovered a beautiful golden flask—the same one the emperor had found in the ashes.

Súmac took the flask and kneeled at the water's edge. Just then a hissing voice behind her said, "Get away from my lake or I shall wrap my long, hairy legs around your neck."

Súmac turned around. There stood a giant crab as large as a pig and as black as night.

With trembling hands the child took the magic fan from her waistband and spread it open in front of her face. As soon as the crab looked at it, he closed his eyes and fell down on the sand in a deep sleep.

Once more Súmac started to fill the flask. This time

With trembling hands, the child took the magic fan from

she was startled by a fierce voice bubbling up from the water.

"Get away from my lake or I shall eat you," gurgled a giant green alligator. His long tail beat the water angrily.

Súmac waited until the creature swam closer. Then she held up the fan. The alligator blinked. He drew back. Slowly, quietly, he sank to the bottom of the lake in a sound sleep.

Before Súmac could recover from her fright, she heard a shrill whistle in the air. She looked up and saw a flying serpent. His skin was red as blood. Sparks flew from his eyes.

"Get away from my lake or I shall bite you," hissed the serpent as it batted its wings around her head.

her waistband and spread it open in front of her face

Again Súmac's fan saved her from harm. The serpent closed his eyes and drifted to the ground. He folded his wings and coiled up on the sand. Then he began to snore.

Súmac sat for a moment to quiet herself. Then, realizing that the danger was past, she sighed with great relief.

"Now I can fill the golden flask and be on my way," she said to herself.

When this was done, she held the flask tightly in one hand and clutched the fan in the other.

"Please take me to the palace," she said.

Hardly were the words spoken, when she found herself safely in front of the palace gates. She looked at the tall guard.

Sumac gave the prince a few drops of magic water

"I wish to see the emperor," Súmac uttered in trembling tones.

"Why, little girl?" the guard asked kindly.

"I bring water from the magic lake to cure the prince."

The guard looked down at her in astonishment.

"Come!" he commanded in a voice loud and deep as thunder.

In just a few moments Súmac was led into a room full of sadness. The emperor was pacing up and down in despair. The prince lay motionless on a huge bed. His eyes were closed and his face was without color. Beside him knelt his mother, weeping.

Without wasting words, Súmac went to the prince

and gave him a few drops of magic water. Soon he opened his eyes. His cheeks became flushed. It was not long before he sat up in bed. He drank some more.

"How strong I feel!" the prince cried joyfully.

The emperor and his wife embraced Súmac. Then Súmac told them of her adventurous trip to the lake. They praised her courage. They marveled at the reappearance of the golden flask and at the powers of the magic fan.

"Dear child," said the emperor, "all the riches of my empire are not enough to repay you for saving my son's life. Ask what you will and it shall be yours."

"Oh, generous emperor," said Súmac timidly, "I have but three wishes."

"Name them and they shall be yours," urged the emperor.

"First, I wish my brothers to be free to return to my parents. They have learned their lesson and will never be false again. I know they were only thinking of a reward for my parents. Please forgive them."

"Guards, free them at once!" ordered the emperor.

"Secondly, I wish the magic fan returned to the forest so the sparrows may have their feathers again."

This time the emperor had no time to speak. Before anyone in the room could utter a sound, the magic fan lifted itself up, spread itself wide open, and floated out the window toward the woods. Everyone watched in amazement. When the fan was out of sight, they applauded.

"What is your last wish, dear Súmac?" asked the queen mother.

"I wish that my parents be given a large farm and great flocks of llamas, vicuñas, and alpacas, so they will not be poor any longer."

"It will be so," said the emperor, "but I am sure your parents never considered themselves poor with so wonderful a daughter."

"Won't you stay with us in the palace?" ventured the prince.

"Yes, stay with us!" urged the emperor and his wife. "We will do everything to make you happy."

"Oh thank you," said Súmac blushing happily, "but I must return to my parents and to my brothers. I miss them as I know they have missed me. They do not even know I am safe, for I came directly to your palace."

The royal family did not try to detain Súmac any longer.

"My own guard will see that you get home safely," said the emperor.

When she reached home, she found that all she had wished for had come to pass: her brothers were waiting for her with their parents; a beautiful house and huge barn were being constructed; her father had received a deed granting him many acres of new, rich farm land.

Súmac ran into the arms of her happy family.

At the palace, the golden flask was never empty. Each time it was used, it was refilled. Thus the prince's royal descendants never suffered ill health and the kingdom remained strong.

But it is said that when the Spanish conqueror of the ancient Incas demanded a room filled with golden gifts, the precious flask was among them. Whatever happened to this golden treasure is unknown, for the conqueror was killed and the Indians wandered over the mainland in search of a new leader. Some say the precious gifts—including the golden flask—are buried at the bottom of the lake at the end of the world, but no one besides Súmac has ever ventured to go there.

The Tree Goddess

A TALE TOLD BY THE ESMERALDA INDIANS OF COLOMBIA

Although the Esmeralda tribe and language are extinct, tales are still told, by their Spanish conquerors, about this unusual tribe of Indians who once thrived on the western coast of Colombia and Ecuador. In these regions of great forests and lively volcanoes, the Esmeraldas were skilled weavers of cotton cloth and inspired molders of elaborate ceramics. Many fine examples of their art still remain, and may be seen in various museums throughout the world. Among these priceless treasures are pieces of gold and silver jewelry. These were used as mountings for exquisite emeralds, from which this tribe derived its name. The beautiful green stones are still being mined from the earth throughout the territory of the Esmeralda Indians of Colombia.

Long before man began to keep a calendar, the Earth was ruled by god Ches. In those days, the lakes were great inland seas, and the fish that spawned there were as large as whales. The animals that came down from the hills to drink at the water holes were enormous in size and fearful in disposition. The jungles, too, were massive, and

82

overgrown with tangled vines. Everything grew wild.

It seemed that the small forests bordering the mountain peaks were the only places of peace and beauty. The trees grew in an orderly fashion and were the most exquisite shade of soft green imaginable.

After man came to live on Earth, the larger animals considered him their worst enemy. They left the hills and went into the jungle to live and hide. A few of the animals made their way up to the mountains and invaded the lovely forests. They ate the leaves and pine cones, and then began to eat the bark off the tree trunks. Many of the forests were devoured and destroyed. Those that remained began to lose much of their green luster.

All of this did not go unnoticed by god Ches, who ruled the world from his seat in the heavens. He was greatly disturbed.

One day the Goddess of the Trees approached Ches.

"Oh, Ches!" she said, "is there no way we can keep at least one forest as it is now? Soon man will put away his bows and arrows and will hunt for beauty. I would like him to see my trees as fresh and new as when I put them there."

"That is not possible," replied god Ches, "for all things must change on Earth." And without further explanation, he turned away.

The Earth did go through many dramatic changes. There were great rains and floods in which both man and beast perished. Only those animals that escaped to the

"Is there no way we can keep at least one forest as it is?"

high forests survived. These became gentler. They also learned to stay out of the clearings and caves where man had taken refuge.

The people who were saved were thankful and, for the first time, turned to the gods in prayer.

When the Goddess of the Trees heard the cries of men, she took pity and gave them the power to see her beauty. But she bemoaned the fate of the lovely green trees that were constantly changing and fading with time. Yet she dared not approach god Ches, for she knew that once he had spoken all must obey.

As she wandered safely through the sky, she saw the Goddess of the Grotto coming toward her in great excitement.

"I have seen the wonderful gift you have given to the people on Earth," she said. "You have made them very happy. They now awake with the sunrise and kneel to look at the sunset. They sit by the brook and listen for the small creatures that have grown wings and live in your trees."

"But alas," interrupted the tree goddess, "the people will never remember my trees as they once were, so rich and green in color!"

"Yes they will," the Goddess of the Grotto assured her, "for that is why I have come."

"What do you mean?" asked the tree goddess.

"I offer you my grotto as a gift to the earth people. Use your magic wand and change the white walls to the vivid green color that your forests used to be. The people can come to the grotto and see things as they once were. Your green color will be preserved forever!"

The tree goddess was overjoyed.

Without saying a word to anyone, the two goddesses left the heavens and flew quickly to the cavern that the Goddess of the Grotto had hollowed into the mountain. How mysterious and beautiful it was! Its many chambers were divided by walls of hard, white, shining crystal that dazzled like the frozen snow on the great mountain peaks.

"Oh, my sister," said the tree goddess, "I cannot cover up all your handiwork. I'll transform only one or two of the inner chambers with my wand."

And so she did. When she had finished, the two goddesses took hands affectionately.

"See how beautifully the velvety-green shines, just as the sunlight does, filtering through the branches of trees," exclaimed the Goddess of the Grotto. "I shall call this green ice Emerald, after you, dear Goddess of the Trees."

At that very moment there was a sudden clap of thunder.

"God Ches is angry!" cried the tree goddess fearfully.

The walls of the grotto shook and rumbled.

"I will go with you to god Ches and ask him to visit the grotto. He will be pleased with what we have done," said the Goddess of the Grotto.

So off they went, and none too soon!

From the safety of the sky they saw the caverns burst their walls and shower their crystals over the world.

"I shall call this green ice Emerald, after you"

Then came five days and nights of rain, flooding the Earth once more. When the rains stopped, not a sign of the grotto remained.

It was later learned that god Ches had indeed become angry because he had not been obeyed. But before many more years passed, god Ches relented. When the people formed friendly tribes, he showed them where they could find some of the emeralds deep in the earth. The Indians made the green crystals into beautiful jewelry that they cherished, for they learned from their wise men that the emeralds were a gift from the Goddess of the Trees.

The Magic Eagle

A TALE TOLD BY THE TIMOTEAN INDIANS OF VENEZUELA

The Timotean Indians once lived in the Andes
Mountains in Venezuela. There, in the sixteenth century,
they built heavily fortified towns which were often populated
with as many as four thousand inhabitants. In the center of
each village stood a temple built in honor of the various gods
they worshipped. Of these many gods, Ches was considered
supreme. He was supposed to dwell on mountain peaks and
in lakes. It was customary for the Timotean ruler and priests
to carry many offerings to these places. Strangely enough, it
was not uncommon for women to become chiefs and warriors of this tribe, but only the men were permitted to become priests and enter the temples. The Timoteans are now
extinct, but there are still traces to be found of their terraced
lands and irrigation ditches, once supplied by ingenious
water-storage tanks.

One day long, long ago, god Ches left his home in the sky
and came to Earth to bestow on his favorite chieftain a
rare and beautiful gift. It was an eagle made of solid gold.
So skillfully designed was this bird that it seemed to be
almost alive.

The chieftain took the eagle in his strong hands. He looked at it in awed silence. Overwhelmed, he could find no proper words with which to thank the god for favoring him over the chieftains of other tribes.

God Ches understood the chieftain's silence and said, "Because of your goodness and wisdom, you alone are worthy of this honor. This golden eagle is not only beautiful, but it has magical powers that will bring your tribe victory in battle and good fortune in times of peace. Guard the eagle and keep it safe until I ask for its return."

The chieftain answered humbly, "Oh, great God Ches, I hope my tribe and I shall always deserve your kindness! When you want the eagle back, only give us a sign and the golden bird will be returned at once."

And so it came to pass that for generation after generation, the god's gift brought victory and good fortune to the tribe. The golden eagle was passed on from one noble chieftain to the next.

Years passed, and still the god Ches had not asked for the return of this cherished possession.

Finally, an unusual event took place. It had never before happened in this tribe's history. A young and beautiful princess became the ruler, for it was the law of the Timotean Indians that a daughter could succeed her father if there were no sons.

Because the princess was wise and beautiful, she was accepted by both the men and women of her tribe. They were proud of her just rule. They loved her kind and gentle ways.

The golden eagle passed from one chieftain to the next

Although she looked fragile, she was as strong as the little hummingbird whose dainty wings can carry it on long flights. Though her close friends sometimes worried about her frailty, they were sure that no harm could ever befall their beloved princess.

Nevertheless, she had not ruled for many moons before she became ill—so ill that the witch doctors were powerless to drive away the terrible affliction that threatened her life. They spent hours making special brews and medicines, while priests burned sacrifices to god Ches on the altar.

In desperation the people painted their bodies red

and danced until they fell from exhaustion. They pleaded with god Ches to spare their princess.

Still there was no answer, and the tribe sat helplessly as the princess grew weaker each hour.

One morning, long before sunrise, the princess awakened from a restless sleep. She called weakly to her dearest friend and companion.

"Mistafá," she whispered, through fever-parched lips, "god Ches has given me a message in my sleep. He asks that the golden eagle be returned at once to his temple on the mountain peak."

Mistafá was certain that the fever had caused the princess to be confused. However, to soothe her, she answered, "It was only a dream, dear princess."

"No, no," cried the princess, "it was no dream! But I am too weak to return the eagle myself, so it is you who must go for me. When it is returned to god Ches, I shall be cured."

Poor Mistafá! She was filled with doubts and fears. Even if what the princess said was true, how could she dare to approach the sacred temple? Only the chieftain could visit the mountain peak. How would she find her way through the forests and canyons?

So she sobbed to the princess, "But how can I find my way?"

The princess held out her hand weakly and replied, "Do not be afraid, dear friend, for god Ches will protect you and show you the way. Now take the eagle from beside my bed and go at once. When you reach the mountain peak, bury the bird at the side of the temple and call three times to god Ches. He will hear and give an answer."

Mistafá saw the princess close her eyes.

"I do not wish you to die, my princess," she cried, "and though I fear for my life I'll gladly go and deliver the eagle."

The princess looked at her friend and smiled. "Do not fear, for we shall both be saved."

Mistafá took courage from these words and, with the precious eagle wrapped in a soft woven cloth of black and gold, she started on her journey.

Each mile her burden grew heavier, until she had to rest more and more often to catch her breath. But each time she arose with renewed strength. When at last Mistafá saw the mountain peak in the distance, her spirit danced within her and suddenly her feet seemed to carry her like wings up the steep road to the top. Only then did she sink down on a rock to rest her weary legs.

The journey had taken most of the day and Mistafá was eager to do her errand and return to the princess before darkness came.

"I must hurry," she said to herself.

Using a sharp rock, she dug a hole at the side of the temple. With tears streaming down her face, she buried the precious eagle that had been her tribe's dearest possession over the long years. Would she ever see it again?

She thought of the dying princess and called loudly three times, "God Ches! God Ches! God Ches! Oh great

She buried the eagle, the tribe's cherished possession

spirit, receive the golden eagle which the princess asked me to return to you, and spare her life."

Mistafá prostrated herself on the ground, overcome by her emotions and by this sacred place. All was quiet.

When she finally lifted her head, Mistafá saw that it was dark and realized that she had fallen asleep.

"How long have I slept?" she asked herself fearfully. "I dare not venture down the mountain until daybreak or I shall lose my way. Besides, I must wait for a sign from god Ches."

She found protection between two large boulders. She wrapped herself in the black and gold cloth in which she had carried the golden eagle. Safe and warm, she fell asleep once more.

When daylight came, she awakened with a start. For a moment she could not remember where she was. Then she saw an unusual sight.

There, in the spot where she had buried the eagle, was a fully grown bush with green leaves and purple blossoms. As she approached the plant, Mistafá was startled to hear a voice coming from the bush.

"Gather my leaves in the black and gold cloth and bring them to the priests of your tribe. Instruct them to make a strong hot tea and serve it to the princess."

"It is the sign from god Ches," Mistafá cried joyfully.

Without a moment's delay, she picked dozens of leaves from the plant, but did not disturb the flowers. She left those to beautify the temple.

She gathered the cloth together in careful folds, and held it tightly under her arm as she descended the mountain. She ran through the forest without stopping to rest. At last she could see the homes of the villagers.

Mistafá hurried the rest of the way until she fell at the feet of the princess, to whom she told what had happened.

The princess called the priests, who wasted no time in preparing the strong brew.

All through the night the princess took sips of the tea. By morning her lips had regained their color and her eyes were as sparkling as ever. The fever was gone.

In just a few more days she had regained her health and was able to make the journey to the temple to thank god Ches for the new plant that had restored her health.

According to the ancient tale related by the Timotean Indians, this plant, known as *Dittany,* first grew high in the Andes Mountains of Venezuela. It has since spread across the seas and is now used throughout the world as medicine. The precious oils from its blossoms are used in the blending of exotic perfumes.

The Disobedient Giant

A TALE TOLD BY THE CUNA INDIANS OF PANAMA

When the Spaniards landed in Panama in the sixteenth century, they found the country inhabited by many Indian tribes. One of the most important was the Cuna, a highly civilized people, proud and fiercely independent. To escape Spanish rule, the Cuna left their ancient homeland in the central part of the isthmus. One group fled to the impenetrable jungles between the Panama Canal and Colombia. The other group settled in Panama's San Blas Islands in the Caribbean Sea. In these areas, their descendants live today, independent of the white man's ways of life, which they consider inferior to their own.

According to tales told by the Cuna Indians, the region of Panama was once a level plain, only slightly higher than the sea. It was easy to plant and cultivate corn and other vegetables there. And, since everything grew out in the open, wild berries were easily accessible instead of being hidden in canyons. The sea also provided them with abundant food.

The Indians did not know why god Oba had chosen to make their particular region flat, but in the beginning it did not matter, for the Cunas were happy in their mountainless land.

But, with the first bad winter storm, the winds blew across the plain. There were no hills or mountains to lessen the gale. Huge waves were whipped to a frenzy and tore out of the ocean in a mad torrent. With nothing to turn it back, the turbulent water rolled far inland, destroying many homes and uprooting the crops.

For days the people waited for the winds to cease. But the storm continued. It was not safe for the canoes to put out to sea. No fish were caught. The land was soaked with sea water. The food was uneatable. Before long, the children cried from hunger.

Not knowing what to do, each family gathered within its own group and prayed to Oba for help.

"We must come together as a tribe and pray," said the oldest of the wise men, "for Oba cannot hear our single prayers above the storm."

So, on the following day, all the people trudged farther inland and met on a damp, grassy meadow. Together they stood with uplifted hands and cried in a mighty voice asking the god Oba's help against the fierce storms. Then they sat down humbly and waited for an answer. It was not long in coming.

The oldest of the wise men spoke: "Oba hears our prayers. He is sending his son, the giant Ologuitur, to help us."

The people rose as one, shouting and cheering, calling out thanks to Oba. How joyous they were as they returned to their water-soaked houses and fields, for they felt safe and secure, knowing that god Oba would help them.

Meanwhile, in the heavenly heights, Oba sent for his son, Ologuitur, who was asleep on a ponderous white cloud. As usual, he left all of the work to his older brothers. It was only because the giant son looked as if he had nothing to do that Oba chose him to go down to Earth to help the Cuna Indians.

When Ologuitur was awakened by his father's messenger, he was grumpy and made the heavens rumble with his yawning and growling. He reluctantly left his soft bed and appeared before Oba.

When the son heard of his task, he scowled. "Get one of my other brothers to go, Father. I'd rather stay here."

"You must go at once, for the others are already busy. Now leave without another word!" commanded his father.

Although Ologuitur knew he dared not disobey, he took his time in making the journey. Therefore, the storm continued for several days and the land became more waterlogged than ever.

When at last Ologuitur reached Earth, he found it difficult for one of his size to tread the wet ground without sinking waist-deep into the mud.

The giant plowed through the wet seashore, then through the ruined corn fields, until he found the great rocks that marked the boundary of the Cunas' land.

There, in the adjoining territory, lay thousands of mammoth boulders. They covered the countryside as far as the eye could see.

"Aha!" cried the giant, "these rocks will make an easy task of it for me! I'll simply roll enough of them over the plains to the seashore and make a mountain high enough to turn back the water."

While he was thinking out his plan, the storm continued to grow worse.

"It's too uncomfortable to work now," he mused. "I'll go back to the sky and return later, when the wind has died down and the waves are calm."

So Ologuitur returned to the heavens, hoping to wait out the storm on a comfortable downy cloud. But Oba stood at the entrance of his home, wearing a stern frown.

"Why have you not helped the Earth people?" he demanded.

"It will suit me better to wait until tomorrow, when the weather is clear," the son replied with an indifferent air. "Then I'll go back and build hills and mountains for them."

"You'll return now!" roared the father angrily. In a rage, he grabbed his son and flung him back toward Earth.

Down, down, tumbled the giant, tearing through clouds and scattering the winds. As he collided with a rainbow, it temporarily broke his fall, but on he went with the speed of a great meteor until he was driven into the center of the Earth.

Down, down tumbled the giant, tearing through clouds

Fortunately for Ologuitur, the ground had been so softened by the continuing rain that he received only slight bruises and scratches.

When his head stopped spinning, the giant looked around. All was dark. There were no heavenly stars. There were no white clouds to sleep upon. There was no moon to guide his way. Even though he was a giant, Ologuitur was afraid.

"I must find my way out of this dark place," he said, groping around.

He stood up tall and strong and started searching for an escape. He walked on and on, stopping to rest from time to time, for he was not used to the weight of the Earth on his head and shoulders.

Far above Ologuitur, in the land of the Cunas, strange events were taking place. The earth trembled. Hills and mountains appeared over the once level plain. Slowly but surely the storm died down, beaten to a halt by these new barriers.

The wise men of the Cunas gathered together and they learned—although no one knows how—that Ologuitur, son of Oba, was bringing about these miraculous changes on the Earth's surface. Mountains were formed while he was walking. Hills rose up when he sat down to rest.

The Cuna Indians of today believe that Oba's giant son still dwells far below the Earth. Although he no longer makes hills and mountains, he often causes the Earth to tremble and shake. He does this as he crawls on all fours

He causes the Earth to tremble and shake, as he crawls

through the dark underground passages looking for the light.

   After centuries of searching, he still has not found his way out of the Earth. Sometimes, when he calls for help, his roars burst through the top of the mountain, and his breath comes steaming forth, causing a volcano. His voice often frightens the Indians, but nevertheless they will always be grateful to him for their beautiful hills and mountains.

Mister Frog's Dream

A TALE TOLD BY THE NICARAO INDIANS OF NICARAGUA

Only a small percentage of the total population of Nicaragua is pure Indian. Before the arrival of the Spanish, however, Nicaragua was inhabited by several Indian tribes, the most powerful of which was the Nicarao. These agricultural people lived on the shores of Lake Managua. Stone images and ancient temple sites have been found on several islands in this lake. This suggests the existence, in early times, of a high civilization, but the Nicarao Indians no longer exist as a tribe.

The Nicarao Indians prided themselves on the care of their hair. They decorated it in many ways, and adorned it with combs. A man shaved his head in various fashions to indicate his social position and his success in battle. Both men and women wore earrings.

Until the arrival of the Spaniards in 1519, the Nicarao Indians were superstitious and practiced witchcraft. After a peaceful encounter with the Spanish, the king of the Nicarao Indians and several of his subjects accepted baptism. In return, the Spanish leader named the land Nicaragua, after this great Indian chieftain, Nicarao.

Ages ago there lived, in a pond near Lake Managua, a handsome young frog who had many talents. He could jump farther, swim faster, and sing more sweetly than any other frogs who inhabited the pond. So highly respected was this gifted creature that his friends and relatives addressed him as "Mister" Frog.

This encouraged the frog to add unto himself another accomplishment—that of speaking.

Of course he had always been able to talk, but only in a modest, quiet way. Now he spoke loudly and almost unceasingly, and always about his own achievements, which he considered spectacular.

Before long, even the most patient grew weary of Mister Frog's harangues and avoided him as much as possible. Determined to have an audience, Mister Frog sought out birds who paused for refreshment at the pond during their long migratory flights. Unlike the frogs, these birds were entertained and amused by Mister Frog's speeches. They encouraged his noisy boastings. Of course they did not have to listen day and night, for they would stay but a short while before joining their companions in the sky.

Soon the summer ended. All the birds had flown south. Mister Frog welcomed the winter, but he missed his audience. However, he was quite exhausted from his efforts and was glad to hibernate in the mud at the bottom of the pond until spring.

One morning Mister Frog was awakened by the chirping of many birds. He rose from his muddy bed and swam to the top of the pond, stretching his legs as far as they would reach. He saw that the sky was blue and the sun bright and warm. It was spring.

Mister Frog ordinarily would have leaped enthusiastically but instead he remained strangely quiet. He had no desire to jump or swim or sing. Neither did he wish to talk. He sought out a fresh lily pad and sat on it contemplating. He only nodded to the other frogs who surfaced the pond after their long sleep. Occasionally, out of need and habit, his sticky tongue would dart forth to capture a meal of insects, but he didn't really relish the food. Mister Frog's mind was on something else. The frogs and birds wondered why he remained so quiet.

Mister Frog was obsessed by a dream he had had while sleeping through the winter. He had seen himself in grand escapades. But the most startling part of the dream was that he had seen himself flying to strange ponds in faraway lands. So real did this flight seem that Mister Frog found himself examining his body for visible means of flying. Alas, he was disappointed to find that he still had only four legs which could get him no more than a short distance from the ground.

He breathed a heavy sigh, which could be heard throughout the pond. This brought his perplexed friends and relatives around him. They knew something was troubling him, and they hoped to be of help.

"Mister Frog, what is the matter?" asked one of his cousins.

All Mister Frog needed was an invitation to speak, for he had not lost his habit or enthusiasm for chatter. It

"I had the most wonderful dream anyone ever had!"

had been a long time since he had such an audience and
he made the most of this opportunity.

He sat up regally and exclaimed, "I had the most
wonderful dream anyone ever had! Come hear about it!"

Although the others knew there would be no stopping him, they chorused politely, "Do tell us what you
dreamed!"

"You'll hardly believe it," said Mister Frog gazing skyward—pausing to add to the suspense—"but I dreamed
I was flying through the sky like a bird." Suddenly Mister
Frog's face brightened as though he were inspired. "Yes
. . . yes . . . I was flying like a bird, and NOW I know
how I can really do it!"

"Wonderful! Stupendous!" the frogs cried. "Tell us
how!"

"No, I shall not!" answered Mister Frog haughtily, "for as you know, there is no frog my equal. Only I can fly."

With these boasting words, Mister Frog took a flying leap off the lily pad over the heads of the others and landed at the edge of the water. There he called to some birds resting in the trees.

"Good morning, Swallow," he cried, "are there any ducks farther down the pond?"

"We do not know," answered the mother swallow, who was busily feathering her nest. "Ask the chorlos, who have come from Argentina. They would have passed that way."

The chorlos, resting nearby, heard and replied in unison, "We are sorry, Mister Frog, but we did not stop to look. We are on our way to the North Pole. The journey is long, so we must be on our way at once." And off they flew, their wings causing a rustling through the air.

Poor Mister Frog was disappointed. He was wondering what to do next when overhead he heard the harsh *cua, cua, cua* of two wild ducks. They swooped down and lighted on the water beside him.

While they were quenching their thirst, Mister Frog swam hurriedly toward them, calling greetings to his old friends.

"We're glad to see you again, Mister Frog," they said. "Did you sleep well this winter?"

"Very well," Mister Frog answered. He was so concerned with his mission that he neglected to inquire how they had fared during the winter. Instead, he blurted out

"I dreamed that you took me flying through the air!"

excitedly, "I dreamed that you took me flying through the air! Will you help me make my dream come true?"

The ducks laughed goodnaturedly. "How can we do this?"

"I remember exactly how it was done in my dream. First, we must find a firm reed. Then, each of you will take one end in your mouth, I shall hold on to the center with my strong upper teeth, and away we shall go. That's just the way I dreamed it."

"Where do you want to fly?" asked one of the ducks.

Mister Frog considered a moment. "Could I go to your summer home?" he asked.

"That's too long a trip," the ducks answered. "But we will take you over the pond several times and maybe over the adjoining fields."

"But I want to go to other ponds in faraway lands!" he cried.

"It will be too burdensome for us," said the ducks impatiently.

"Very well," agreed Mister Frog quickly, for he was afraid they would fly off and desert him. He had hoped for a longer trip, but on second thought he decided that if the flight were viewed by all the creatures in the pond, it would provide more for him to brag about.

"One thing you must remember," cautioned the older and wiser duck, "under no circumstances must you speak during the flight."

"I know that!" advised Mister Frog with an air of importance. "I always know what to do!"

While Mister Frog searched for a suitable reed, the news of his flight spread quickly.

Everyone assembled to see the takeoff.

Each duck took hold of the reed and Mister Frog grasped the center with his mouth. They left the ground and circled just above the water. Then up and down they swooped over the heads of the ogling creatures in the pond.

Never had Mister Frog been happier. Never had he felt more brazen. He wished he could fly forever!

Mister Frog could not help but notice how pleased the two ducks were with their performance. He felt a wee bit jealous that they should be stealing some of his fine act. He saw they were enjoying the praise from the on-lookers just as much as he was, so he thought: "Perhaps

They left the ground and circled just above the water

now they will take me with them. We will be the talk of the ponds and meadows wherever we go!"

Each time the ducks flew around the pond they became more and more daring. They boldly swooped faster and faster, whirling Mister Frog until he became too dizzy to think.

"Slow down . . ." he pleaded.

Alas! With these words he let go of the reed and fell from the sky.

A gasp of horror came from the crowd below him. They scattered in every direction. Some took to the shore. Others dove for safety to the bottom of the pond.

Mister Frog tumbled round and round and then went headlong into the pond.

The large splash sent ripples right to the water's edge. The lilies bobbed. The cattails bent low with the unexpected tide.

When everything stilled, there was Mister Frog, the wind knocked out of him, floating on the water. His ego was really deflated.

The first of his cousins who reached his side asked, "What happened?"

Mister Frog would not look at him, but simply answered, "I just don't want to talk about it."

And he didn't.

How the Porcupine Outwitted the Fox

A TALE TOLD BY THE MAYAN INDIANS OF HONDURAS

One of the greatest civilizations in the Americas was that of the Mayas, who flourished between 300 and 1500 A.D. Their descendants still live throughout southern Mexico, and in the Central American countries of Guatemala, Honduras, and El Salvador. Most of them are now corn farmers. But centuries ago the Mayas were fine architects and artists. Ruins of Mayan stone-built cities attest to their greatness. Their skilled astronomers invented a calendar which was just as accurate then as the one we use today. A method of writing and a number system were also created by their scholars. One of their most interesting pastimes was a game called "Pok-ta-Pok"—a combination of handball and basketball that may well have been the basis of those games as they are played today.

Long, long, ago a family of porcupines lived in the great evergreen forests of Honduras. Because of their timid nature, they lived a lonely life in a secluded section of the woods. But they were content and happy.

Although the porcupine has changed little in habit

since the beginning of time, he has changed greatly in appearance from the creature first created by the great god Noh Ku.

Early one summer evening, Mr. and Mrs. Porcupine climbed down from the poplar tree, where they had been feasting on tender bark and juicy twigs, and began shuffling their way home. Suddenly Mr. Porcupine stopped. He sniffed the air and a pleased expression came over his face.

"Do I smell fresh clover?" he asked hopefully. He sniffed again and his eyes brightened. "Yes, it is! Let's go to the meadow and eat some before we go to bed."

"We've just had a fine meal," replied his wife. "Besides, we should be aware of the hungry foxes who hide in the tall grass."

"It is too late for foxes to be hunting for food. You go home if you wish, but I must have a few nibbles of clover leaves."

"Oh, very well," sighed Mrs. Porcupine. And she returned alone to the great pile of rocks that was their den.

In the meadow, Mr. Porcupine nibbled the sweet-smelling clover. Each bite led to one more, and he could not seem to satisfy his appetite. Faster and faster he ate and farther and farther into the meadow went Mr. Porcupine until he was a considerable distance from the edge of the forest. But he had nothing more on his mind than his stomach, so you can imagine his sudden fright when he heard a movement in the grass ahead of him. He strained his eyes to see. Then, as the moon appeared from behind a cloud, it lit up a shadow crawling slowly across the meadow.

It was the sly fox!

"It's the fox!" screamed the porcupine in terror, and looked around for a tree to climb. But of course none was near and there was no time to dig a hole in which to hide. Mr. Porcupine knew it was useless to try to outrun the fox. How then could he save himself?

"Help me, Noh Ku," he cried in panic, "please save me from the fox!"

The long shadow of the fox came closer and closer. The porcupine huddled in fright. Suddenly a cold chill, and then a strange feeling, ran through his flesh. Something was happening to the coarse hair that covered his back!

At that moment the fox sprang from the ground and pounced upon his prey.

A painful howl was heard across the meadow.

The fox dropped the porcupine and ran whimpering in pain back into the forest.

Mr. Porcupine was left trembling. He could not understand his good fortune. He only knew that somehow the god Noh Ku had answered his plea for help.

Without another moment's delay, Mr. Porcupine wobbled back to his den.

Mrs. Porcupine was still awake. Her fears for her husband's safety had kept her from sleeping. When she saw her husband, her eyes opened wide in amazement.

Suddenly a strange, cold feeling ran through his flesh

But before she could speak, he gasped breathlessly, "I'm home at last, but only because the good god Noh Ku has protected me."

"But dear husband, what has happened to your brown coat?" she asked.

"What do you mean?" Mr. Porcupine answered in a puzzled voice.

"Come with me to the brook and look at your image in the moonlit water," she answered. "Then you will understand."

When they arrived at the water's edge, Mr. Porcupine looked at his reflection. He could scarcely believe what he saw! Instead of his coat of short hair, he saw dark quills with yellowish-white tips all over his back.

At last he understood that the god's gift was this unusual coat of armor. Now he could venture into the meadow and out of the trees any time he wished, fully protected against his enemies.

So happy was the porcupine with his new coat that he could scarcely keep from dancing a jig. But he noticed that Mrs. Porcupine did not share his jovial mood. She stood with her head lowered, not making a sound.

"Are you not happy about my miraculous escape from the fox? Am I not lucky to have been given such a coat?" Mr. Porcupine asked.

"Of course I am glad you were saved, but nevertheless I feel very sad," she answered softly.

"But why?" asked her husband in a bewildered voice.

"Well," she began slowly, "without a coat to protect me, I will not be able to accompany you on your trips to the meadow." Suddenly she began to weep. "Besides," she wept, "you look as if you belong to another family!"

Mr. Porcupine did not know what to say. Had god Noh Ku punished him for his foolish need to satisfy his appetite? Would he bring nothing but sorrow to his loved ones? What was he to do now?

Suddenly he opened his mouth and gasped in surprise.

"Look at yourself in the water!" he shouted to his wife joyfully. And she did.

"Why I have a coat just like yours!" she exclaimed.

"I believe," added Mr. Porcupine wisely, "that this night god Noh Ku has given all in our family a new coat like ours."

Mr. Porcupine was right. From that day until the present time, all members of the porcupine family have been born with quills like those given to their long-ago ancestors by the good god Noh Ku.

The Peacock and the Puhuy

A TALE TOLD BY THE MAYAN INDIANS OF EL SALVADOR

The peacock was not always so beautifully plumed as he is today. However, in long-ago times, he was able to sing so melodiously that all the birds—even his nearest rivals, the lark and the nightingale—marveled at his exquisite trilling and his clear high notes.

But it was not enough for the peacock to *sound* beautiful; he wanted to *look* beautiful. He thought it was most unfair that he should be endowed with a glorious voice, yet be forced to wear a coat of dull, dingy feathers. To make matters worse, these feathers were tattered and frayed, and no amount of preening could make them smooth or shiny.

In those days, it was not unusual for the gods, who ruled from the sky, to come down to Earth for a visit. So it was that one fine day Chaac, God of the Birds and Fields, made his appearance in a clearing in the great forest. When news of his arrival reached the birds, they flew in haste to greet Chaac, for they loved him dearly.

After the hubbub and excitement died down, each

bird made himself comfortable on a roost and waited with polite respect for god Chaac to speak.

"The time has come," Chaac announced to his audience, "for you to choose another leader and relieve King Eagle of the duties he has performed wisely and well for such a long time."

The eagle bowed so low in appreciation that he almost toppled from his lofty perch in the tallest pine tree close by. Regaining his balance, the eagle thanked Chaac for the compliment and asked, "When shall we hold the election?"

"Tomorrow morning when the sun touches the mango grove, you will all gather to cast your votes. Then you may have the rest of the day for festivities in honor of your new king."

Hardly had Chaac finished speaking, when many of the birds began to chirp loudly—especially those aspiring to be king.

"Choose me," hooted the owl. "I will make a wise king."

"Wisdom alone is not enough. A king should be able to fly high and see great distances in order to know what is happening in his kingdom. That is what I can do best!" screeched the buzzard.

"Nonsense!" pooh-poohed the cardinal. "Choose one who *looks* like a king. Is not my scarlet coat most regal in appearance?"

God Chaac lifted his hands and silence fell upon the forest. He slowly waved his arms and the birds departed in an orderly fashion.

Through all this chatter, the peacock had remained silent. He seemed to be listening, but in reality he was working out a scheme to further his own ambitions. After god Chaac had dismissed the birds, the peacock lost no time in putting his plan to work. He flew at once to find the puhuy.

The peacock found this timid bird blissfully sunning himself in front of his nest.

"Good day, friend Puhuy," called the peacock. "I have come to ask a favor of you."

Although the puhuy was endowed with feathers of rare beauty, he was far from proud. Indeed, the puhuy was so bashful he seldom ventured more than a few yards from his home. Only two or three other birds besides the peacock befriended him.

"What is the favor, friend Peacock?" the puhuy asked shyly.

"First, don't you agree that I have all the qualifications for being a king?" questioned the peacock.

"Of course," answered the puhuy quietly, not daring to say otherwise.

"But I will not be elected king simply because of my dull feathers," moaned the peacock. "Now if I could adorn myself in your fine coat, all the birds would give me their vote. Won't you let me borrow your coat until after the election tomorrow?"

Since the puhuy was a trusting creature, he was unable to see falsehood in his friend. So he said, "Very well. But when will you return my coat?"

"You shall have your coat again after the festivities,

of course!" The peacock tried to make his words ring
true. But his tone of voice did not matter, for the puhuy
was too innocent to recognize trickery.

"In return for your kindness," the peacock continued,
"you shall share the honors of my office with me."

The puhuy removed his splendid coat of dazzling
green and gold tail feathers. The peacock fitted it on himself, holding the feathers in a high fanlike arch. He
adjusted the beautiful collar of blue pinfeathers at his
throat. He set the fragile crest of plumes upright on his
head. What a magnificent sight the peacock was as he
strutted about in his borrowed finery!

So pleased was he, and so vain had he become, that
the peacock never stopped to thank the puhuy. Nor did he
notice that the poor naked little bird had run to hide in
the nearby bushes.

"Friend Peacock," the puhuy called from his hiding
placc, "I shall remain in these bushes out of sight until
the festivities are over. I will not leave until you return
my coat."

"Do as you wish," replied the peacock as he practiced
strutting up and down in a regal fashion.

The puhuy lowered his head and eased himself further back into the shrub.

Without saying another word, the peacock marched
away into the forest.

The next morning all was in readiness for the election. In the center of the clearing stood Chaac and, at his
side, were the birds who hoped to be chosen king. The
bushes and lower branches of the surrounding trees were

"I shall remain in these bushes, out of sight"

weighted down with hundreds of excited birds eager to cast their votes.

Suddenly a lovely song was heard in the distance. It was the peacock. A great hush fell over the forest. Nearer and nearer came the song. Then out of the thicket walked the proud peacock, timing his steps to his carefully chosen notes. He marched stately and tall, his tail feathers raised high. Even the god gazed in awe at this magnificent creature.

"Here is our king!" the birds cried in one voice. "The peacock must be our king!"

Without delay, Chaac proclaimed the peacock king of the birds and signaled for the festivities to begin.

How proud the birds were of their handsome king!

The celebration continued for several days longer and the vain peacock could think of nothing but his victory.

Meanwhile, the puhuy dared not come out for food or water until night fell to cover his nakedness.

One evening the god Chaac saw the poor bird at the water's edge. When he saw the puhuy without a coat, he questioned him. As soon as Chaac learned of the peacock's falseness, he was determined to punish him. But first he provided a modest covering for the puhuy.

"I have clothed you in this way," explained the god with a gentle reprimand, "so no bird will ever wish to take advantage of your shy and generous nature again."

But the puhuy knew he was being punished for his foolishness and returned to hiding in the bushes. He was determined never to be seen in his poor attire. The jeers and taunting of his few friends would be more than he could bear. Besides, the puhuy still felt that somehow, someday, the peacock would return his fine coat as he had promised.

As for the peacock, the god Chaac punished his falseness by taking away his gift of song. In its place he left the peacock with a harsh, piercing shriek. Of course the peacock was no longer able to wear the king's crown!

We do not know why Chaac permitted the peacock to continue wearing the puhuy's fine coat. Perhaps he hoped that the peacock, of his own accord, would return the coat to its rightful owner. But so far, he has not done so, and the puhuy continues to stay out of sight as much as possible.

The Sacred *Amulet*

A TALE TOLD BY THE QUICHÉ INDIANS OF GUATEMALA

More than one half of the people of Guatemala are full-blooded Indians. They are descendants of the ancient Mayan Indians and of a kindred tribe, the Quiché. At present, most of the Indians make their homes in rural villages in the highlands, where they live much as their ancestors did. Each tribe, and almost every village, has a distinctive costume. Designs have not changed in hundreds of years. The Quiché language is spoken by all the Indians, although some have learned Spanish. Most Quiché villages have witch doctors who try to cure illness by magic and witchcraft. They foretell the future, and protect the people from evil gods. The Quiché, like their Indian neighbors, are proud, dignified, and industrious.

Except for the chieftain, the most important member of the Quiché tribe was the soothsayer. A soothsayer was similar to people who today call themselves fortune-tellers.

Because everyone believed the soothsayer to be inspired by the gods, no one ever doubted his words. Neither the chieftain nor the wise men of the Quiché tribe made any decision without consulting him. He prophesied regarding the weather. He foretold the future.

Often the soothsayer made strange predictions, and none was more strange than the one you are about to read.

It happened many years ago that a son was born to the powerful chieftain of the Quiché tribe. He named the boy Quetzal.

At the time of the child's birth—as was the custom—the soothsayer was summoned to predict his future.

There was much festivity. But when it came time for the soothsayer to speak, there was not a whisper in the room. Everyone listened to him with awe and eager anticipation.

"This youth," the soothsayer began, "will be loved and admired by the tribe for his skill and bravery." He paused a long time before continuing. "His future is unusual—most unusual. But I am not permitted to reveal that secret until the next prophecy is due. When Quetzal becomes of age, only then I will tell what his future holds."

As time went on, Quetzal became everything the soothsayer had predicted. He excelled in hunting, fishing, and in all tests of endurance. He never lacked courage. He was gracious and good. He also had the wisdom and understanding of a grown man while he was still a child. Was it any wonder the tribe held Quetzal in great esteem and affection?

The years passed swiftly by and soon Quetzal would be of age. Then he could take part in the council meetings that were attended by his father, the wise men, and the soothsayer.

One morning Quetzal went to summon his father for such a meeting. Much to his grief he discovered that the old chieftain had died quietly and peacefully in his sleep. Of course the whole tribe was shocked and saddened and tried as best they could to console the young son. Meanwhile the council met to declare the new chieftain who, of course, would be Quetzal.

After a brief period of mourning, the tribe began to prepare for the festivities in honor of their new leader. Several days later, the celebration began.

Musicians appeared clad in robes of purple and scarlet. Some performed on wooden drums. Others blew weird sounds on ancient clay pipes. A gaily decorated marimba was placed close to where Quetzal sat, and a tribesman played his favorite songs. There was joyful dancing and much feasting throughout the night.

As the first rays of golden light appeared, a hush fell upon the crowd. Up stood the royal soothsayer with his hands held high. From one of his wrists dangled a strange object. It appeared to be an amulet, or good-luck charm. After chanting several words of praise to the gods the soothsayer placed the necklace around Quetzal's neck. He then spoke loudly and clearly so that all might hear his words.

"Quetzal is now of age and has become our chieftain.

When he was born I spoke of a great secret that I could not reveal until now. Let it be known that his future is forever protected by the gods. They have decreed that Quetzal shall never die. He will live forever through all generations of Quichés."

There was a loud cry of joy and thanksgiving from the people. Everyone fell to his knees and humbled himself in front of Quetzal whom the gods had chosen to honor. Everyone, that is, except Chiruma who was Quetzal's wicked uncle. Chiruma stole away to brood by himself.

Now it should be told that Chiruma was only slightly older than his nephew Quetzal. And he had hoped that Quetzal's life would be short so that he himself might become chieftain. But how could his dream come true if Quetzal was going to live forever?

Chiruma sat with his face in his palms and began plotting and scheming to bring about his young nephew's downfall.

Suddenly an alarm was sounded, calling all the Quiché warriors into action. A warlike tribe from a nearby village was taking advantage of the Quiché celebration and was attacking them.

Although this was Quetzal's first experience in battle, he fought courageously and well. It was a short, fierce, battle and the Quiché tribe was victorious. This was due to Quetzal, who placed himself at the head of his warriors. Each time the enemy's arrows were aimed, as if by magic they were turned aside and fell to the ground. Of

Without awakening Quetzal, Chiruma lifted the blanket

course the attackers fled in terror, for they thought some witchcraft was at work.

But Chiruma knew better. He was certain that Quetzal was protected by the amulet the soothsayer had placed around his neck. Chiruma was determined to lose no time in stealing this magic object.

That night while Quetzal lay sound asleep, his scheming uncle stole into the room. Without awakening the young chieftain, Chiruma lifted the blanket and saw the tiny feather of a humming bird hung as an amulet around Quetzal's neck. Chiruma quietly drew out his hunting knife and cut the deerskin cord on which the feather hung. Then, palming it tightly in his hand, he stole out of the room.

"This is the powerful amulet," said Chiruma joyfully as he prepared for rest. "Now we shall see if Quetzal will live forever."

The next morning Quetzal discovered his loss. He was frantic. Without waking another soul, he ran into the forest where the soothsayer lived. Quetzal was sure that if anyone could help him, the soothsayer could. But unfortunately Quetzal was being followed by the wicked Chiruma. This evil man had not rested. His theft made him all the more wary of his nephew. When he saw Quetzal take the path in the woods leading to the soothsayer's house, Chiruma feared that his awful deed would be revealed.

Taking a shortcut through the forest, Chiruma reached the soothsayer's dwelling before Quetzal. He stayed hidden behind a tree.

When Quetzal was but a short distance from the soothsayer's home, he heard the fluttering wings of many humming birds. He stopped to look and listen. But their warning came too late. The whistling sound of an arrow pierced the air. Quetzal cried out; then he sank to the ground, holding his bleeding chest.

The soothsayer heard the disturbance, but was too late to save Quetzal. He saw the cruel uncle fleeing the

forest and shouted after him: "You have stolen the amulet, but its magic belongs only to Quetzal. It will not
protect you."

But Chiruma did not hear.

When he reached the village he spread the story that
one of the enemy had ambushed the young chieftain in
the forest.

"We were hunting together," mourned Chiruma,
shedding false tears, "and my brave nephew protected me
with his own life!"

Of course you must be wondering why the soothsayer
remained silent. It was because he knew the gods had
their own way of punishing Chiruma. And they did. But
that is another story.

As for Quetzal, the gods kept their promise. They
changed him into a beautiful bird that still dwells in the
forests of Guatemala. Its body is as green as the grass on
which the youth breathed his last, and its breast is the
color of blood. Its blue-green tail is three to six feet long
so it can hang low from the limbs of trees and be easily
recognized.

Before the soothsayer died, he revealed the story of
the Quetzal bird. And, ever since, the bird has been considered sacred and cannot be hunted. In Guatemala today
they honor this royal creature by putting its image on the
national coat-of-arms. Indeed, even the coin of the country is called the quetzal.

So, as was predicted so many long years ago, the
young chieftain lives on forever.

The gods kept their promise and changed him into a bird

The Cuckoo's Reward

A TALE TOLD BY THE MAYAN INDIANS OF MEXICO

Long ago, many different gods ruled over Yucatan, a region in southern Mexico. Some were wise and good. Others were spiteful and unkind.

One of the wisest and most loved was Chaac, God of the Fields and Crops.

On a bright, spring morning Chaac called all the birds to a meeting in the woods. "As you know," the god said, "the time for planting is at hand. Will all of you help me prepare the fields as you have in other seasons?"

From the trees came many sounds, among them the gentle voice of the dove, the harsh squawk of the eagle. They agreed to help, each in his own way.

After the birds became quiet, the owl—counselor of the birds—asked in his dignified way, "When shall we start our work, god Chaac?"

"Tomorrow at sunrise," the god answered. "But you must work quickly, for at midday the fire god will come to burn off the old plants."

Before Chaac had finished speaking, the cuckoo fluttered from bird to bird. Her bright yellow eyes and plumage of rainbow colors caused many to look at her in admiration.

"What must we do?" she called loudly. "Will some one please tell me? I cannot remember what I did last season."

The owl was ashamed of the cuckoo's bad manners. "You cannot remember because you never came to help us. But this season we expect you to do your share."

"She hides because she is afraid of fire," screeched the parrot.

The cuckoo became silent. The parrot had spoken the truth. Fire did frighten her, although she was sure the parrot spoke against her because he envied her gay feathers and beautiful song. Many said she sang as well as the skylark and the nightingale.

God Chaac smiled, and raised his hand for silence. "I am certain each of you will do your part. The task is simple. Each bird is to collect his favorite seeds, along with many grains of corn. These are to be piled near the woods, so they can be planted when the fields are ready."

Long before the sun came peeking over the land, the owl—who had spent the night on a tree stump in the woods—was awakened by crackling noises. He flew quickly to a tall tree, and, just as he had suspected, there were fires nearby. In the distance, he saw the fire god scampering from field to field, setting everything ablaze with his great torch.

"This is another of the fire god's spiteful tricks,"

There was one lone bird flying through the flames

thought the owl, as he winged his way through the woods to arouse the other birds. "Quick! Quick! Fly to the fields!"

Over and over he called. When the birds and god Chaac reached the scene, they could not believe their eyes. There was one lone bird flying back and forth through the flames.

"Surely it must be a heavenly bird," they chorused, "for no earthly bird is endowed with the courage and strength to bring out seeds from such a fiery place."

"It has smoke-colored feathers," observed the owl.

"No, the feathers are colored gray from the smoke," answered god Chaac.

The bird was so tired it now turned away from the burning fields, and flew to a pool where it eased into the cool water.

"It is the cuckoo!" the birds cried. "The brave cuckoo!"

The voice of the parrot was louder than any of the others.

All the birds gathered around her in wonderment, for she had saved the seed that would furnish food in the winter ahead.

The owl spoke in his wise, kindly way: "Dear Cuckoo, as a token of our love, we wish to grant you and all cuckoos an everlasting reward. From this day on, other birds will care for your children and your children's children down through the ages."

So that is how the cuckoo got her gray feathers and flame-colored eyes, and why she puts her eggs into the nests of the other birds who will raise her young.

Bird Cu

A TALE TOLD IN MEXICO

The giant Ahuehuetes, or cypress trees, that grow in Mexico City have been there for more than a thousand years. Once they were part of a forest that bordered on a vast lake. Today most of the forest and the lake have disappeared. In their place stands a great city.

It is often said that in the stillness of the night, when the big city sleeps, the Ahuehuetes whisper to each other of days long past. There are so many unusual stories they remember.

One of these stories is about Bird Cu.

Bird Cu once made her home in one of the Ahuehuetes. She was a kind neighbor and a loyal friend, but she had one very unpleasant habit. She complained to everyone about her ragged gray feathers.

"They make me look so ugly," she cried.

On ordinary days she complained about her feathers ever so little. On fiesta days, when she saw gay-colored birds dancing and singing, she complained more often.

But it was at the great reunions that she complained the most. Then the birds came from far and near, their

138

beautiful feathers carefully preened and brilliant with color. On seeing them so beautiful, Bird Cu moaned and cried and wailed so loudly that she made a great nuisance of herself.

When the next reunion time came around, the birds gathered in the forest for their meeting. As usual, the eagle served as their leader.

He had only begun to speak when Bird Cu cried out in a loud voice, "Oh, oh, oh! How ugly I am! Why can't I have gay feathers like the parrot, or peacock, or quetzal?"

The turtledove flew to her side and spoke gently. "You know the good god Tonotuih made all of us birds. He knew the kind of feathers each of us should have, so you must not complain."

But Bird Cu went right on complaining, even though other birds came and tried to comfort her.

Finally, the eagle, not able to make himself heard, flew over to talk with the owl. "You are wise. Can you tell us how to help poor little Bird Cu?"

"Let me think," answered the owl. He closed his great round eyes and kept them closed so long that the eagle thought he might have fallen asleep.

When he opened his eyes at last, he said, "It really is very simple. Little Bird Cu wants gay feathers. Is it not true?"

The eagle replied that it was true.

"Then we shall give her gay feathers."

"Give her gay feathers," repeated the eagle. "But how? Please explain to all of us."

"Can you tell us how to help poor little Bird Cu?"

Then the owl spoke quickly, fearing that Bird Cu might start complaining again and drown out his words. "Bird Cu can have beautiful, gay feathers, if each bird will do his part. Are you birds willing?"

"I will do my part," cried the parrot.

"Gladly," said the peacock with dignity.

"Of course," added the quetzal.

"I will! I will!" shouted all the birds. Their words rang out through the great forest until it sounded as if the trees were speaking and saying, "I will! I will!"

Bird Cu, sniffing loudly, said she wanted to do her part, too.

"Then come with us, Bird Cu," said the eagle as he flew with the owl to the foot of a tall pine tree.

While the other birds watched from the trees, the eagle covered Bird Cu from her beak to the tip of her tail with thick, sticky pitch from the pine tree.

Now the owl spoke. "Each of you is to pluck a bright-colored feather from your body. Then fly down and press it into the pitch on Bird Cu."

In no time at all, little Bird Cu was covered with such pretty feathers that she was the gayest-colored bird at the reunion. She was as beautiful as a rainbow.

Still perched under the pine tree admiring herself, she cried out, "Oh, how grateful I am to all of you."

The birds were happy for her; that is, all except the eagle. He was anxious.

"She is grateful *now*," he said to the owl, "but suppose she becomes proud and vain? That must never happen!"

The owl closed his eyes again, but he did not keep

them closed so long this time. He said, "Give her work to do and she won't have time to admire herself. Make her a messenger for all the birds. In that way she will be helping those who helped her."

Bird Cu was very willing. "I shall be the best messenger there is," she promised, and she meant it at the time.

What a flash of gay plumage she was as she darted across the sky, delivering her messages with speed and courtesy! But just as the eagle had feared, in time she became proud and lazy. She became rude, too, speaking sharply to everyone, even to the eagle and the wise owl.

Then the time came when she flew to a hiding place and stayed for several days so she could avoid having to deliver messages.

One day the eagle came upon her and said, "Before the storm god sends the great rains to our thirsty earth, we must have another reunion. Go speedily, Bird Cu, and spread the news from the hot desert to the damp jungle, and on to the faraway ocean where the gulls ride the tossing waves."

"Sir Eagle, I will go at once and carry out your commands."

The eagle was pleased with the courteous attention and polite reply given by Bird Cu. He thought, of course, that she would keep her promise.

On the day of the reunion, the eagle, proud and noble, soared down from his home on the mountain crag, eager to see the birds who would be waiting for him in the Ahuehuetes.

But no birds were there. Not one!

"Have they disobeyed? Or have they forgotten? In any case, there is no excuse for their absence," thought the eagle.

Away he flew over the Great Pyramids and went swiftly to the jungle, then to the desert, and then far away to the restless ocean. And as he flew he called to all the birds.

"Why are you not in the Ahuehuetes, as you were commanded to be? Hasten, and no excuses," he cried.

The eagle's strong wings were weary by the time he returned to the reunion. However, even when he was searching for a place to light in the Ahuehuetes, he could hear the other birds chirping in anger.

"We are accused of disobedience! It is that lazy, ungrateful Bird Cu who is at fault! She never told us of the reunion! She is the one who should be punished and the owl should be punished, too, because he gave such bad advice in asking us to give our feathers to Bird Cu. Now she is vain and lazy! It is he who is responsible."

The eagle was deeply sorry then that he had scolded the birds when they were not to blame. When he had quieted them, he said, "God Tonotuih made all of us, so now let us ask him what punishment should be given to Bird Cu and the owl."

From the sky the voice of god Tonotuih thundered down to them.

"The birds are so angry that I fear some harm may come to Bird Cu and the owl. So, from this day on until all the birds can forgive them, they will become night birds. They will sleep during the day and come out only after darkness falls and the other birds are sound asleep."

And that is just what befell Bird Cu and the owl.

Many, many years have passed since god Tonotuih gave his command. Now all of the birds have forgiven Bird Cu and the owl and are eager to see them again.

So, any day now, perhaps even while you are reading this tale, Bird Cu and the owl may cease being night birds and may fly joyfully out into the warm sunshine again.

The Ahuehuetes are certain the time is near at hand. On still nights, in Mexico City, it is said that one may hear them singing softly:

> *You are forgiven, good wise owl,*
> *And dear little Bird Cu.*
> *Come back to the sunshine again,*
> *Where we'll all welcome you.*

Printed in U.S.A.